Praise for

RUTH: THE WOMAN WHO FOUND ROMANCE IN A BARLEY FIELD

"Exciting, entertaining, and educational. Ruth: The Woman Who Found Romance in a Barley Field *is all of these and more. Relationships supersede 'the letter of the law' throughout the story. I liked the good words about Grandmother Rahab."*

—John Sawyer
>Retired Director of Discipleship Training,
>Alabama Baptist Convention

"This delightful book by Vona Elkins, which fictionalizes the story of Ruth and Boaz, is scripturally based and full of insight from ancient Bethlehem-Judah and Moab. The illustrations are well-drawn and correlate with the story nicely. An overall, enjoyable read."

—Jennifer Hallmark
>Co-author of the *Heart Seekers* series

"Intriguing and riveting. The beautiful story of Ruth is told in a fresh and compelling manner. The exquisite illustrations by Ruth Bochte help to make this book a treasure. Many of the chapters led me to self-examination. I realized that in many areas of my life, I am like the frog Boaz described to Elimelech."

—Art Criscoe, Ph.D.

Retired Director of Discipleship and Family Youth/Children/Preschool Department, LifeWay Christian Resources

"I was deeply blessed as I read the story of the life of Ruth; I was reminded of God's providence and faithfulness to those who believe in Him. I thought I knew the story of Ruth, as I have read this book in the Bible many times. But it just came alive for me as Vona revealed details of the culture and more about their day-to-day life and conversations. I highly recommend this book. It is brief and will leave you wishing it was longer."

—Amy Boone

Executive Director/Treasurer of the WMU of North Carolina and the author of *Stones from the Riverbed*

"Vona Elkins gives me a new understanding of loyalty because of the way Ruth reacts to the situation she is in. By reading this book, I'm convinced that Ruth showed more maturity than her age would suggest. The story of Ruth that Ms. Elkins portrays should inspire us to face the challenges in our own future with hope and determination."

—Jerry Sibley
Author of *The Adventures of Harley Earle* series

"The book of Ruth is one of the world's great short stories. I like the way Vona Elkins amplified it, particularly her use of dialogue to both develop the characters and to keep the narration moving. The novella is very well-done, and I can see youth groups, Bible study groups, and Sunday school classes reading it with interest. Readers of the Bible will appreciate its dependence upon scripture. It rings true."

—Nancy Whitt, Ph.D.
Professor Emerita of English,
Samford University

"*Vona Elkins' novella about the story of Ruth has forever altered my perception of this much-loved and often-referenced Old Testament book. The Cinderella story of an unexpected but clearly God-driven romance certainly comes alive through Ms. Elkins' fictional retelling. Her attention to detail— emotional, relational, and physical—grips the heart and challenges our minds to think past what we believe we know to a setting that 'might have been.' Her creative portrayal of a time and place and events that moved history forward for the Jewish people leaves us once again aware of the undeniable fingerprint of God's sovereignty in the affairs of this nation—even as His people were watching and waiting for the revelation of their Redeemer.*

"*Ruth's growing faith, her rescue by Boaz her kinsman-redeemer, and the events leading to Naomi's joyful gift of a grandson, bring fresh hope to all who wait for redemption from suffering.*"

—Lettie Kirkpatrick Burress

Author of *Glimpses of Grace: Stories of Hope* and *Taking Back Christmas and Other Family Celebrations.* Contributor to *Home Life* magazine and *Journey*

"Here in the story of Ruth is a timeless truth— that of a God who manages to grant us blessings from undeserved places. Vona Elkins has written the story of Ruth and Boaz in a faithful and faith-filled way, encouraging her readers to understand God's covenantal faithfulness to His people and His undeniable blessings upon those who care for the widows, the foreigners, and the poor. This God of second chances has a unique plan and purpose for our lives, one that He alone can fulfill and manage, and this classic biblical story is a victorious illustration of that truth.

"My favorite quote: 'Don't ever think of yourself as being less than someone else, my dear. You are who God created you to be. You can't let your family history control your destiny. He has a plan and a purpose for your life.' *Boaz to Ruth."*

—Andrea White
Teacher and Composer of Music

"Vona Elkins creatively used her skills to provide an easy-to-read story that will encourage you. You will be reminded that blessings often come from the places we least expect."

—Phil Waldrep
CEO of Phil Waldrep Ministries
Author of *Reaching Your Prodigal: What Did I Do Wrong? What Do I Do Now?*

"Beautifully written, deeply moving, the message powerful. The author must have had an angel on her shoulder as she wrote, reintroducing us to one of the Bible's most beloved characters with a storytelling technique that will both surprise and inspire you."

—Jack D. Smith
Author of *My Father the Ghost*

"Vona brings to life the love story of Ruth and her kinsman-redeemer in this timely message for the church and all followers of Jesus Christ today."

—Tanya Shearer
Multiple contributions in *Chicken Soup for the Soul*

"One generation will
commend your works to
another;
they will tell of your mighty
acts"
(Psalm 145:4, NIV).

DEDICATION

This novella is dedicated to the loving memory of my parents, Buford and Earline Brackin. From them I learned at an early age about the grace of God and the importance of prayer. Their prayers still carry me.

In memory of my brother, Buddy Brackin; I miss our family sing-a-longs around the piano.

And to the loving memory of Billy Clark Elkins, husband and father of our three children.

To my children: Andy, Beth, and Penny, and their spouses . . . grandchildren: Chad, Chase, Kristin, Cortney, Bekah, Kelsey, their spouses, and Kaitlin . . . the great-grands: Collin, Chloe, Aubrey, Cooper, and those yet to be . . . Only God loves you more than I do.

When you need comfort, forgiveness, or joy on your journey, be encouraged by the story of Ruth. God has plans and purposes for your lives. Trust Him. . . .

I ask myself . . . Will I just be a fond memory to those I encounter on my journey, or will my life have lasting significance through a word spoken, or written, or witnessed from my life of attempted faithfulness to God because of His faithfulness to me?

Let it be so, dear God . . . my Savior and my Lord.

RUTH

THE WOMAN WHO FOUND ROMANCE IN A BARLEY FIELD

VONA B. ELKINS

RUTH: THE WOMAN WHO FOUND ROMANCE IN A BARLEY FIELD

Copyright © 2017 by Vona B. Elkins

ISBN-13: 978-0692913598
ISBN-10: 0692913599

Published by:
GO-EL Publishing
256-810-7961
vona256@charter.net

Scripture taken from the HOLY BIBLE, NEW INTERNATIONAL VERSION ®. Copyright © 1973, 1978, 1984 by International Bible Society. Used by permission of Zondervan. All rights reserved.

Cover, interior illustrations, and formatting: Ruth Bochte
Author photo: Two Girls And A Camera Photography

Order additional copies through GO-EL Publishing.
Printed by CreateSpace, an Amazon.com company.
www.CreateSpace.com / 7293861
Printed in the United States of America.

⁊

MY GIFT TO:

FROM:

*"From the fruit of his mouth a
man's stomach is filled;
with the harvest from his
lips he is satisfied"*
(Proverbs 18:20).

Table of CONTENTS

"I will instruct you and teach you in the way you should go; I will counsel you and watch over you" (Psalm 32:8).

FOREWORD

The story Vona Elkins shares with us here, from the Book of Ruth, not only gives us insight into the woman whose story God's Word has so beautifully preserved, but it also gives us insight into the heart of the author and the God she serves.

In this telling of *Ruth: The Woman Who Found Romance in a Barley Field*, Vona has taken us within the pages of scripture to help us see ourselves in the characters of that day.

In it, we discover a family not unlike our own: a man who longs to provide for his wife and children; a wife and mother determined to honor her God and her husband; two sons who strive to make a home for themselves in a foreign land. But as with families today, this one does not face these challenges alone. Instead, others' lives become interwoven with their own to form the tapestry that is God's plan in action, and the result has far-reaching implications, even for us today.

My relationship with author Vona Elkins is something of a tapestry too. We live in different states and always have, but God has orchestrated it so that our paths have crossed throughout the years in a variety of ways. It has been a blessing to witness God at work, bringing our lives together—for encouragement, instruction, and fellowship. I can't wait to see what else He has in mind for our friendship because our deepest connection is that of sisters in Christ.

If there is one thing I know about Vona Elkins, it is that she—more than anything else—desires to lead others to Jesus, just as Naomi, by God's grace, led Ruth to the kinsman-redeemer. And, like the characters in this narrative, Vona has experienced life's unexpected challenges, the loss of loved ones, the joy of hope, and the beauty that comes from submitting to the will of Almighty God. In fact, this work is evidence of that.

It is with this in mind, that I bid you go into these pages and see what God has in store for *you*.

—Beth Henderson
Writer, friend, and fellow-laborer for Christ

"Let this be written for a
future generation,
that a people not yet
created may praise the
Lord"
(Psalm 102:18).

INTRODUCTION

Inspired by the Word of God in the Old Testament book of Ruth, this fictional retelling of recorded events follows an early Hebrew family living in the "Promised Land" of Canaan. The story opens in the little town of Bethlehem in Judah during the time of the judges. It was a time when most people rejected God and did what was right in their own eyes. Much turmoil existed in the land.

As you read this book, you will find unforgettable narratives of faith and friendship, loss and love all within the legacy of Elimelech, a man who struggles with conflicting loyalties. You will discover that our choices often have eternal consequences that affect not only us but future generations.

True to one of the most beautiful love stories of all time, Ruth, a young widow and stranger to the covenant people of God, finds salvation and hope. In God's providence, she finds love in a barley field. God blesses her marriage and makes her an ancestor of the Messiah who comes into the world centuries later.

Through Ruth, God demonstrates His redeeming love for all humankind, giving hope and purpose to life.

We are assured that God has a plan for each person. He is *God* and can work in any way He chooses and work in any *one* He chooses to bring about His eternal will and purpose on the earth.

*"As long as the earth
endures,
seedtime and harvest,
cold and heat,
summer and winter,
day and night
will never cease"*
(Genesis 8 :22).

Chapter 1
FAMINE IN THE HOUSE OF BREAD

"In the days when the judges ruled, there was a famine in the land" (Ruth 1:1).

Elimelech walked out his door into the early morning sunrise. As far as his eyes could see, there was only parched, dusty land . . . land that was someday to become his sons' land . . . land that once flowed with "milk and honey." He meandered down toward what was once a lake. It was now a tiny puddle. He looked up toward the heavens.

"Where are You, God? You promised that You would be our God and that we would be Your people. You promised never to leave us or forsake us."

The crackle of dry leaves alerted Elimelech to the fact that he was not alone. He turned around.

Boaz stood there with a smile on his face. "Shalom, cousin Elimelech. This is the day the Lord has made; let us rejoice and be glad in it!"

Elimelech sighed. "What's there to rejoice about, Boaz? Just tell me."

"Well, the early morning sunrise for one thing."

Elimelech shook his head. "Don't you see that puddle of water out there? I remember when there was enough water in that lake to water all the livestock around here with some left over. No, I'm sorry, but I don't see a lot to rejoice about. I go to bed worried and get up worried. I go out to check for signs of rain and come back to a rain of tears."

Boaz moved a step closer and laid a hand on Elimelech's shoulder. "Why the tears?"

"Oh, you know how children are. Those boys of mine are worried about their dog. Ole Shadow doesn't run and play with them like he used to. This dry, hot weather doesn't help any."

"Their concern doesn't surprise me," Boaz said. "They say a dog often becomes a man's best friend, and I'm inclined to believe it. It's plain to see how much Mahlon and Kilion love that dog. Wherever you see them, you see Shadow."

"They've had him since he was a pup. Naomi and I never worry about the boys' safety when Shadow is with them. I don't know how much longer we'll have him with us though. It's ironic, isn't it? We have a sheep dog but no sheep. This famine has taken care of that."

"I'm afraid there's a much worse famine among us, Elimelech, a spiritual famine, a famine of the soul. Many people have turned away from God, but that doesn't change who He is. He's the same yesterday, today, and forever. Even in trying times, we need to continue to trust His promises."

Elimelech shook his head and mumbled under his breath.

Boaz cupped his ear. "What did you say?"

"I said I *know* what we need. We need *rain*!"

Boaz nodded his head. "I know we do, but it's in God's hands. He has sustained us thus far. I believe He will continue to do so. Remember, He parted the Red Sea to bring our people out of Egyptian bondage."

Elimelech kicked the dry ground. "I wish He had saved some of that water for us today."

"Surely this famine will be over soon," Boaz said. "We must keep the faith, my friend. We don't want to be counted among those who have contributed to our nation's decline and decay."

"That's easy for you to say. You have enough of everything. Bethlehem means *House of Bread*, but my cupboard is almost bare, and the well is almost dry! Another irony: a famine in the House of Bread."

"This famine has taken its toll on everyone," Boaz said in a softer tone of voice. "I understand your frustration."

"I doubt that you do." Elimelech's lips tightened. "You don't *have* children—or a wife—for that matter." Silence filled the air between them. "I'm sorry, but I'm a bit on edge this morning. I have a lot on my mind."

"I understand. I'll be on my way. I see your boys approaching now. Give my regards to Naomi."

"I will," Elimelech said, holding out his hand. "Naomi has high regard for you."

Boaz shook Elimelech's hand warmly. "And I regard her highly. Her parents named her well. Naomi is indeed a pleasant and sweet lady. You are a fortunate man."

"Yes, I know. Have a good day, Boaz. I'm off to the marketplace to see what's available."

As Boaz walked away, Elimelech turned toward his approaching sons.

"Hello Father," two young voices said in unison.

"Hello there, my sons. What brings you out so early in the morning?"

"We've been looking for Shadow," Mahlon answered as Kilion wiped away a tear. "He's been very slow lately. It's plain to see that he is feeling poorly."

Kilion pulled at his father's tunic. "Hear those frogs croaking? They must be thirsty. Look at the cracks in the ground. If we don't get rain soon, I fear Shadow may step in one and break a leg! Maybe he already has."

"Let's hope not, Son. You boys don't need to be out in this sweltering heat too long." There was concern in Elimelech's voice. "Run along home now. I see Shadow approaching; take him with you."

"But Father, we want to go to market with you," Mahlon protested.

"Not today, boys, but someday soon we'll go on a real adventure, maybe to a faraway place." Elimelech looked beyond what was left of the lake toward a distant country.

"And Shadow," Kilion asked, "can he go with us?"

"Certainly, Kilion. Now run along and tell your mother I'll be home soon."

Elimelech walked to the marketplace and hurriedly gathered up what he could of what they needed. With an expression of turmoil on his weathered face, he started back home. He had a decision to make—one that was keeping him awake at night—a decision that was making an old man out of him.

"Hello there, Elimelech, how are you, my friend?"

Elimelech turned around. "Oh hello, Adley . . . hello, Liora. How are you?"

"We're doing alright, but how about you? You seem a bit preoccupied, my friend."

Elimelech shrugged. "A little, perhaps."

"And where is Naomi?" Liora asked. "I had hoped to see her today. Her smile is like a ray of sunshine in a dark world, or better yet, like water in a dry land." She chuckled.

"I wish—" Elimelech said. "Excuse me. I must be on my way."

Elimelech dared not look his neighbors in the eyes for fear they would see the truth. He walked away. He had struggled with sleepless nights long enough. His mind was made up. He had a plan. He would leave Bethlehem and move his family to Moab.

"*Moab*," he muttered. He found it hard to speak the word. Moab was a pagan land that God had forbidden the Israelites to enter. It was a land that did not honor or worship the one true God—the God of the Israelites. They bowed their knees to false gods.

"But what am I supposed to do? I have Naomi and the boys to consider," he said to himself.

As Elimelech retreated, Adley shook his head. "I wonder why Elimelech was in such a hurry."

"Didn't you see that dejected look on his face?" Liora asked. "Something is wrong in that household. Elimelech is not his usual self, or Naomi either, now that I think about it. I must pay her a visit. Perhaps she needs a listening ear."

"I believe you're right, Liora," Adley said with a frown on his face. "Wait for me here at the market-place. I want to catch up with Elimelech. I'd like a private conversation with him."

"Hey, wait up, Elimelech! I wish to speak with you for a moment."

Elimelech stopped walking. He turned and faced Adley. "I'm listening."

"Something is troubling you, my friend. Would you like to talk about it?"

"No, Adley, there is nothing to talk about. At least nothing you can help with. It's just—well—I have a gut-wrenching choice to make. It has to be my choice, and it is not an easy one."

"Well, I can appreciate your dilemma. It seems life is full of these gut-wrenching choices."

"Yes, my friend, it is. But some choices are made for us, such as this famine we are experiencing. I certainly didn't choose it. Did you?"

"Of course not, but Elimelech, we sometimes have to accept what we can't change."

Elimelech motioned toward a dried up barley field in the distance. "Well, I can't change this famine, but I can change my reaction to it."

"What do you mean . . . change your reaction?"

"Change my reaction to the fact that I'm losing everything I have worked for all my life. I'm getting out of this God-forsaken place. I'm moving my family to Moab where the grass is green, and the fruit is on the vine!"

"Are you out of your mind? We can't just do what's right in our own eyes like the pagans around us. We invite the judgment of God if we do so. We are God's chosen people. You know the land of Moab is filled with idolatry. Remember, God's servant Joshua said: *God forbid that you should forsake the Lord to serve other gods*. I think perhaps this famine we're experiencing is the result of our disobedience to God."

"So now you are presuming to know the mind of God." Elimelech spoke with an edge in his voice. "Well, don't *you* judge *me*. Leave the judging to God. Besides, this move is just a sojourn. This famine will be over someday, and we will return."

Elimelech wiped the sweat from his brow. "Look around you, Adley. This is not living. This is just *existing*. My mind is made up. I only have to tell Naomi." His voice broke. "That's the hard part."

"But Elimelech, I beg you to think of your family heritage—your legacy. The ground you walk on is the land that was promised to Abraham, the father of our nation, generations ago. God gave us this land."

"Then I'll give it back to Him. Only *He* can make something out of nothing."

Elimelech walked away in a state of turmoil. He had a plan—but deep down he knew Adley was right. His plan to move to Moab was not in keeping with the Word of God.

But what else was he to do?

If he stayed in Bethlehem, he stood to lose everything he had worked so hard to accumulate. He had a family to think about. After all, it would only be a temporary move. He was torn between two worlds. There was a famine in the House of Bread, and his mind was pulled toward a better place.

Or was it?

"I can't ignore this another day," she said through clenched teeth. "I have to know the truth. We're in this thing together."

Chapter 2

PLANS WITHOUT GOD

"In those days Israel had no king;
everyone did as he saw fit" (Judges 21:25).

Naomi stood at the door and watched her sons as they returned with Shadow. What joy they had brought to her and Elimelech's lives.

Elimelech was a good father and a good husband. Naomi had felt secure in his love . . . until recently. She was much aware of his tossing and turning in the night. She had seen the despair in his eyes and the weariness in his slumped shoulders as he left the house each morning. Her heart ached for him. He was concerned about the lack of rain, but Elimelech was wrestling with something much deeper than that. He couldn't hide it from her. She knew him too well. He used to share his struggles and his hopes and dreams with her, but not anymore. There was a wall between them. He had pushed her away.

Naomi stepped aside as Mahlon and Kilion entered the house. "Where is your father?" Naomi asked. "Have you seen him this morning?"

"We saw him talking to Cousin Boaz when we were looking for Shadow," Mahlon answered. "Father sent us home, said he had things to do. I think he was headed to the marketplace."

Kilion looked up at his mother. "Mother, do you ever dream of going to faraway places?"

"No, I can't say that I do. I'm content in this place where God has placed us. Things aren't perfect, but we have friends, and we have each other. Why do you ask such a question?"

Kilion answered, "I believe Father dreams of faraway places. He said we might go on an adventure to a faraway place. That would be exciting, wouldn't it?" Naomi remained silent. "Mother! I said wouldn't that be exciting?"

Naomi didn't answer. Her mind was caught in a whirlwind. *Elimelech has dreams of faraway places? What can that mean? He has never mentioned this to me. Had the boys heard him correctly? What was this adventure of which he had spoken? Was that what was keeping him awake at night?*

Kilion spoke again, "*Mother*, did you hear me?" He turned. "Look, I see Father coming up the path."

"Yes. I heard you," Naomi said. "Here, my sons. Return this shawl to Liora. You have my permission to stay and play with Nava and Jaden. Run along now."

Naomi closed the door behind the boys and watched out the window as Elimelech climbed the hill to their house.

"I can't ignore this another day," she said through clenched teeth. "I have to know the truth. We're in this thing together."

"Hello, Naomi," said Elimelech as he came in and laid his purchases on the nearby table. "I saw Adley and Liora at the market. They send you greetings. Where are the boys?"

"I sent them to play with Nava and Jaden." Naomi's eyes grew cloudy. "Elimelech, we must talk. I deserve to know what is going on in that stubborn head of yours."

"Yes, we do need to talk," Elimelech answered without looking into Naomi's eyes.

"What is this tale you have been telling the children about going to a faraway place?" She put her hands on her hips and stepped closer.

"Naomi, you know how hard I've worked and how much satisfaction I have gotten from being able to provide for you and the boys in a generous way. But those days are gone. They ended with the last stalk of grain that died. I want us to move to Moab until this famine is over."

Naomi's jaw dropped as she regarded the man she loved.

Elimelech continued. "There is life in Moab, Naomi. There is work to be had. There is water in the lakes, cattle in the stalls, and fruit on the vines."

"And may I remind you, husband of mine, there is also forbidden fruit! The Moabites live a sensuous lifestyle—and more. They worship pagan gods. They sometimes sacrifice their children to one of their gods. They know nothing of our God. Surely you are not serious about moving to Moab!"

The tension was thick in the room.

"I am. Moving is exactly what I propose to do."

"But what about Mahlon and Kilion?" Her eyes welled up with tears. "Their playmates will be

Moabites. You know how impressionable children are. Bad company can corrupt good character. And what about our family and friends? How will we explain this sojourn to them?"

"Mahlon and Kilion will be *fine*, Naomi. They have each other, and they have Shadow. A healthier diet will make them stronger. You know they both have weak constitutions. This famine won't last forever. When it's over, we'll return." Elimelech looked out the window at the parched fields. "This will be a temporary solution for us. I don't have to raise sheep, you know. I'm a decent potter. I can set up shop and sell my wares like my grandfather did. Wouldn't it be nice, my dear, to enjoy a lifestyle like the one we enjoyed in the past?"

"But you can't expect the blessings of God to go with us to Moab."

He turned around and picked up a bag from the table. "Look at this meager bag of grain," he said, raising his voice. "Do you call this day-to-day struggle a blessing?"

"But we are a covenant people, Elimelech. Our God is the God of Abraham, Isaac, and Jacob. Have you forgotten? Your very name proclaims that Jehovah God is King. How can you walk away from that?"

"Maybe God is in Moab too, and the people just don't know it yet. Besides, we can still worship God in our home, just you and I and the boys. If we stay here, we risk losing everything." He reached out to her. "Please, Naomi, I'm doing this for you and me . . . and those yet to be. Try to understand."

"I understand one thing. You are a stubborn man."

"And you are a beautiful woman. I treasure you so."

"Flattery will get you nowhere," Naomi said with a small laugh. "Don't even try that tactic on me. It won't work this time. The situation is too serious. Please, my husband, won't you reconsider this plan of yours?"

"I've already reconsidered it, Naomi—day and night for a long time. Sometimes a man just has to *do* what he has to *do*. Surely God will understand. My mind is made up. We are leaving the day after tomorrow—so start packing!"

"But Elim—"

"Say no more, Naomi. I have made my decision." He walked out of the house, slamming the door behind him. With the slam of the door, Naomi thought her heart would break.

"Do you ever wonder about the Promised One? . . . Do you think He will come soon? We've been waiting a long time for His appearing."

Chapter 3

TALKING IT OVER

"A man of many companions may come to ruin, but there is a friend who sticks closer than a brother" (Proverbs 18:24).

Naomi walked hastily to her place of solace—a garden to where she often escaped when she needed to pray and meditate on the goodness and mercies of God—a garden that once held the promise of life in the soil, once lush with wisteria and jasmine and food for the table. Nothing was left now but broken dreams. The rains had not come, and everything around her looked as dead as her shattered heart felt. She sat down on a nearby bench.

Time began in a garden, she remembered, a garden of good with evil lurking in the shadows. A sense of foreboding made her shiver. Her tears fell like drops of rain upon the dry ground. She felt a touch on her shoulder and looked up to see her friend Liora.

"Hello, Naomi. I thought I might find you here. What's wrong?"

Naomi raised her head. "Oh, Liora, it's too dreadful to talk about, even with you, my friend."

"That's what friends are for. There's healing in tears, my dear, but no one should have to cry alone. Tell me about what troubles you. I must confess, I have heard some rumors." Liora sat down on the bench beside Naomi. "Adley had a conversation with Elimelech at the market, and he is very disturbed about this plan of his."

"Then how do you think I feel? I can't bear the thought of leaving my family and friends and moving to a pagan land. It is against everything we have always believed in. It is not what I want for myself or my family. But what choice do I have? We know that the husbands make the decisions. Somehow it doesn't seem quite fair. Right or wrong, we too have to bear the consequences of those decisions."

Naomi stood up and looked down at Liora. "Tell me, do you suppose we will always be under a man's authority, not having any rights of our own? Do you ever wonder about the Promised One? Some tend to think He will come as a mighty warrior. Somehow, I think He may be a kinder, gentler person. Do you ever wonder what role we women will play in His kingdom? Do you think He will come soon? We've been waiting a long time for His appearing."

"Hey, slow down, Naomi. I believe God's promises—the Promised One will come, but no, I don't believe we will see Him in our lifetime. But we wait expectantly . . ."

"Liora, you know I have always honored Elimelech's decisions, even when I haven't agreed with him. It has not been burdensome until now because I love my husband and usually trust his judgment, but this time . . ."

"*This* time, he is *wrong*. But if he is determined, and Adley seems to think so, there's not much you can do about it."

Naomi sat down. "You are right about that. Elimelech has a mind of his own. He's never been one to sit around and do nothing. He has always been a man of action. I must admit, however, that the idea of a lifestyle without so many struggles sounds enticing. I haven't had a new shawl in years. And I'm so tired of trying to prepare nourishing meals with so little to choose from."

"I know the feeling." Liora sighed deeply.

"Will you say goodbye to our friends for me, Liora? I hate farewells, even if it is only for a short time. Elimelech says we are to be packed and ready to leave the day after tomorrow. He says this will just be a temporary solution."

"Let's pray he is right." Liora patted Naomi on the shoulder. "I will miss you so. Perhaps Elimelech will yet change his mind. If not, take comfort, my friend. God is not limited by our circumstances or our understanding. His ways are not our ways, and His thoughts are not our thoughts. Keep looking up. Who knows? Maybe God, in His time and in His providence, will bring something good from this sojourn in Moab. Think back to the story of our forefather Abraham and his wife Sarah. God sent them into an unknown territory, and the nation of Israel was born."

"But Liora, God told Abraham to move. He didn't tell Elimelech to move to Moab. He is doing what is right in his own eyes. The history of our people should remind him that disobedience is costly. I wonder if Sarah felt like I feel at the moment, confused, afraid, and yes—I'm angry also."

After Elimelech had issued his ultimatum to Naomi, he left the house and walked for miles. When he slowed his pace, he found himself near the edge of a field belonging to Boaz. He had no desire to talk with his cousin again, but he knew when he heard Boaz' voice, he had waited too long to retreat.

"Hello, Elimelech. The cool of the evening is a good time to walk and talk with God, isn't it? If you have the time, I'd like a word with you."

"Of course, Boaz. I always have time for you."

"You know I am not one to pry into another man's affairs, but you are my friend as well as my relative. I believe I can speak freely."

Elimelech crossed his arms. "I'm listening. Go ahead and speak your mind."

"I heard through Adley that you are contemplating a move to Moab."

"That's right. We'll leave the day after tomorrow. The well-watered strip of land to the east of the Dead Sea is fertile. It provides excellent conditions for farming and raising animals. From what I've heard, Moab is thriving with other business opportunities also. I expect I'll find a way to make a living, maybe even as a potter. I've saved my grandfather's pottery wheel, you know."

Boaz shook his head. "Let me remind you that choices have consequences, eternal consequences . . . oftentimes from one generation to another. I am disturbed by this choice you've made."

The muscles in Elimelech's jaw contracted. "I have a family to feed, Boaz."

"I realize that, but *please* consider the things you are giving up. Your parents guided you and taught you the ways of God. As a child, you learned from their example and from others around you. It grieves me to think of Mahlon and Kilion growing up in an environment like that found in Moab."

"They will be fine."

"What about Naomi? How is she handling this decision?"

Elimelech shrugged. "As you would expect, I suppose. Listen, Boaz, I appreciate your concern, but this move won't be forever. As you said yourself earlier this morning, this famine will be over someday. In the meantime, it is my responsibility to provide for

my family. A man is not much of a man if he doesn't provide for his family."

"I applaud your desire to care for your family, but I just can't keep quiet about this." Boaz pointed to the dried up lake. "Hearing those frogs croak reminds me of something I learned from a man much wiser than me. He said if you drop a frog into a pot of hot water, it will jump out immediately. But if you drop it into a pot of cold water and set the pot on the coals where it heats slowly, the frog will stay there until it dies."

"And?"

"He said we can become desensitized to something that is wrong by gradually adjusting to it. After a while, we become comfortable and find ourselves just blending in and accepting it. Be careful that you don't conform to the pagan lifestyle around you."

Elimelech fidgeted. "I hear what you are saying, Boaz. I'll keep that in mind. I made a pledge to Naomi that I will continue to teach our boys about Jehovah God in our home. Rest assured that I will do so."

"If you are determined to leave, and it seems you are, then please take a pair of my oxen and a cart," Boaz said with sadness in his voice. "It will make the journey much easier for Naomi and the boys. And Elimelech, even though I'm fearful of the choice you have made, I bid you, Shalom. My prayers to Jehovah God will include one for His provision for you and your family." Boaz looked deep into Elimelech's eyes. "*Please* don't tarry too long in Moab."

"I won't. Thank you for your friendship. I hope my sons grow up to be the man you are."

Boaz walked away then stopped and turned around.

"Elimelech! It's not too late to change your mind."

Elimelech didn't answer. He stood at the crossroads of life. All the way home, he seemed to hear the voice of Boaz ringing in his ears. *Elimelech! It's not too late to change your mind.*

The pressure was great.

Chapter 4

THE LONG JOURNEY
AWAY FROM GOD

*"In the days when the judges ruled, there was a famine in the
land, and a man from Bethlehem in Judah, together with his
wife and two sons, went to live for a while in
the country of Moab"* (Ruth 1:1).

After two fitful nights, Naomi awakened early to
the sounds of movement outside her window.
With a sinking heart, she understood what
was happening. Elimelech had not changed his mind.
The day of their departure had arrived. Against the
advice of his family and friends and God Himself, he
would carry out his decision to move his family to the
idolatrous country of Moab.

She looked out the window. The cart was loaded.
She suspected Cousin Boaz had provided the oxen

and the cart. Mahlon and Kilion were jumping up and down with excitement. They had never traveled outside of Bethlehem. Even Shadow seemed excited about this journey.

With an aching heart, Naomi walked out of the house as the boys climbed up into the cart. She preferred to walk. She could not bear to look her husband in the eye.

Dear God, journey with us. Please be faithful, even when we are unfaithful.

"Mother, don't look so sad. We're going on an adventure," Kilion said.

Naomi turned her head away. She refused to let Mahlon and Kilion see her tears. She would accept what she couldn't change. With steel in her backbone, she put a smile on her face, but it didn't reach her heart.

As the cart moved forward, she turned around for one last glimpse at the home she loved. Would she ever feel at "home" again?

The journey was long and tiring. Naomi's feet kept moving forward, but her mind kept racing backward . . .

back to Bethlehem, the House of Bread, back to friends and relatives . . . back to Jehovah God.

The excited voices of Mahlon and Kilion brought her back to the present. "Father, are we there yet? Where will we live? Mother, will we have friends?"

"Look Father!" Kilion pointed ahead. "The trees are getting green. There is a stream. Can we wade in it?"

Elimelech stopped the cart. They all needed a little rest.

"Come on, Shadow, there's water!" Mahlon yelled with excitement.

"I found a fig tree, Father! May we gather some figs?" Kilion asked.

"No, Son. Those trees don't belong to us. Someday soon we'll have figs of our own—and grapes, and bread, and plenty of water. We'll even purchase a few sheep for you boys and Shadow to look after. Come now, we must continue our journey."

Naomi looked into the eyes of Elimelech and saw a spark she had not seen in a long time. She smiled in spite of herself. At that moment, she silently vowed to embrace the ride, enjoy the journey, and cherish every moment with Elimelech and their sons. Life was too short to waste time looking back. She would trust God and leave the consequences to Him.

She climbed up into the cart beside Elimelech and touched his hand. *It is not my right to question my husband's wisdom.*

"Don't grieve so," Elimelech said. He squeezed her hand. "Everything will be alright. Just wait and see."

"Father, what are those strange creatures sitting everywhere?"

Chapter 5

SOJOURNERS IN A STRANGE LAND

"The man's name was Elimelech, his wife's name Naomi, and the names of his two sons were Mahlon and Kilion. They were Ephrathites from Bethlehem, Judah. And they went to Moab and lived there" (Ruth 1:2).

Naomi watched the changing countryside as she traveled with her family. The grass became greener, the air fresher. Could Elimelech be right? Would this move really be a good one?

Finally, they were there. Foreign faces turned their eyes to gaze upon the little family from Bethlehem as they entered Moab.

"Father, what are those strange creatures sitting everywhere?" Kilion asked.

The question sent a chill up Elimelech's spine. He understood the wisdom in the story of the frog. But it didn't apply to him. After all, it would just be a short sojourn.

Shadow barked when two little girls bent down to pet him.

"Look, Mother, we will have some friends our own age to play with," Kilion said with excitement.

"You will have each other as friends, my sons."

The boys didn't heed the warning in their mother's voice. They jumped out of the cart and joined Shadow and the little girls.

Naomi shuddered. *Will my sons someday gravitate toward idol worship?*

Elimelech glanced at Naomi. "Dear God," he heard her pray. "Deliver us from evil, keep us strong, and keep us safe."

With the help of a few people from Bethlehem-Judah who had already established themselves in the town, Elimelech soon found a place for the little family to live.

Naomi started feeling better about the move. "Elimelech, maybe we will have friends here after all."

"We'll see, Naomi, we'll see." He was reluctant to admit to her that most of their people who had come earlier had already conformed to a pagan lifestyle.

It didn't take Elimelech long to construct a place to make and sell his pottery. It blessed Naomi's heart to see him bending over the pottery wheel. There was a spring in his step that was good to see. He was a fine potter, and soon his work became known throughout the region. Someday, he would train his sons to follow in his footsteps.

Mahlon and Kilion's health improved. They were happy to be tending a few sheep. It even seemed Shadow had new life in him.

Naomi often found herself singing as she prepared meals and tended her garden of herbs and flowers. Their little family was thriving and enjoying the fruits of their labor—or so it seemed.

Although life was good, the yearning for home never left Naomi. Every time she came face to face with the ungodly lifestyle in Moab, a cloud of darkness pressed in upon her. Elimelech came to recognize these moods. The questioning gaze she sometimes directed toward him over a meal made him uncomfortable.

"What's on your mind, Naomi?"

"A lot of things, Elimelech. When I look around and see these people worshiping false gods, I think it must break the heart of God. Don't you think the things that break the heart of God should break our hearts also?"

"Where is this conversation leading?"

"I know God instructed us not to intermarry with the Moabite people lest we be pulled away from the one true God, but now that we are here, shouldn't we try to get to know them? How else will they learn about the love of God if we don't show them and tell them?"

"Go on . . ." Elimelech said.

"I heard about a sick Moabite lady when I went to the well to draw water. I'd like to carry her some lamb stew and a bouquet of flowers from my garden."

"Do as you wish. You can put the flowers in one of the vases from the pottery shop if you like."

"Thank you, my husband. I'll do so later today."

When Naomi returned from her visit with the sick lady, she joined Elimelech on their porch. The shadows of night were falling. The sweet aroma of jasmine drifted through the night air. "Where are the boys, Elimelech?"

"They have gone to look for Shadow. They haven't seen him since morning."

"Father! Mother!" Mahlon appeared, breathing heavily. He was holding a dead snake by the tail.

Naomi jumped to her feet, her eyes filled with horror. "Where is your brother?"

"He's over the hillside with Shadow," Mahlon said, choking back tears. "Shadow is dead. He gave his life to save Kilion's life from this ole snake."

The family walked briskly up the hill together. They found Kilion holding Shadow in his arms. He looked up, tears streaming down his face. "What will we ever do without our faithful friend?"

"Give him to me, Son," Elimelech said gently. "I'll lay him to rest." A tear escaped his eye.

Who says weeping is only for the weak in heart?

Months became years.

Naomi had become known in Moab as a charitable person. Giving out of her resources gave her a great sense of satisfaction.

Mahlon and Kilion grew up. The little girls they had come to know as Ruth and Orpah blossomed into beautiful young women. They still smiled when they saw Mahlon and Kilion.

The pottery business prospered. Elimelech never mentioned the subject of going back to Bethlehem. On occasion, a gnawing guilt engulfed him when he remembered his conversation with Boaz. He couldn't forget the warning about the frog in the pot.

When he first viewed the idols and immoral lifestyle in Moab, he experienced shock and guilt for being there, but he soon became accustomed to all the carnality and the sensuous living. . . . *Have I settled for material security instead of eternal security? Am I the frog in the pot?*

True, he still prayed to God and spoke of Him in their home, but it was more from duty and not true worship. There seemed to be a wall between him and God.

Elimelech sat at the potter's wheel. Naomi carried him a dipper of cool water. "Here, my husband, please take a break."

"Thank you, dear." He stepped down from the wheel and moved closer to Naomi.

"I'm grateful I have the opportunity to make my pottery from my own shed," he said. He took a sip of the water she offered him. "This way, I get to see you more often."

Elimelech saw that familiar faraway look in Naomi's eyes. He sat down on a big rock nearby and pulled her down beside him. He rubbed her back.

Elimelech, "Have you heard any news from Bethlehem lately?" she asked.

"From what I hear from travelers passing through, things haven't changed much," he said. "If we had stayed in Bethlehem, we would still be enduring a famine."

Naomi moved Elimelech's hand away and looked him in the eyes. "Have you ever considered the fact that it might be safer to be in the midst of a famine with God than to be in a foreign land with plenty but without God? I'm homesick for friends and relatives with whom we can pray and celebrate our religious feasts, those whose example can teach our sons of our godly heritage."

She sighed. "It's plain to see that most of the other Hebrews who migrated here have already conformed to this ungodly lifestyle. I fear for my family."

Naomi stood and moved beyond Elimelech's reach. "You said this sojourn wouldn't be forever, but it seems like forever to me. I long to see the land of promise."

"Just a little longer, Naomi. Just a little longer."

"But Elimelech, can't you see that Mahlon and Kilion are growing into manhood? They are young men now with the same desires as other young men. Whom will they marry? The young ladies of Moab are known for their great beauty. The boys often work with you in the pottery shop. Surely you have noticed how the young ladies look at them. I've often overheard the boys speaking with fondness of Ruth and Orpah. Look down the street." She motioned. "They are saying good night to them right now! God have mercy if they marry Moabite girls!"

Elimelech turned his head and watched until the boys reached home.

"Oh hello, Father. Hello, Mother," Mahlon said brightly. We didn't see you sitting there."

"Apparently not," Elimelech said. "Why were you out with those Moabite girls?"

"We enjoy their company. We wanted to get to know Ruth and Orpah better," Mahlon said. "All Moabite girls aren't bad, Father."

"Perhaps not, but we are Israelites. We are God's chosen people."

"We haven't heard a lot about that lately, have we," Mahlon retorted.

"Don't you dare be disrespectful to me, Mahlon!"

"Father, please try to understand. I love Ruth, and I plan to ask for her hand in marriage someday. Kilion feels the same way about Orpah. Give them a chance. You'll see they are fine girls."

"They are Moabite girls."

"Well, you don't mind accepting Moabite money for your pottery," Kilion spoke up loudly.

Elimelech's face changed colors. He jumped up and pointed his finger at Kilion. "I've heard enough of this nonsense. We will speak of it no more. In the meantime, you two had better think long and hard about this foolish plan."

Naomi listened quietly to the confrontation between the boys and their father. The spirit of rebellion she saw in her sons' eyes troubled her. What did Elimelech expect? They had always been good boys, but they were in a pagan land with all the temptations it presented. Surely he must understand that.

Dear God, may they not be led into temptation but delivered from evil, she prayed.

"Naomi!" There was panic in
Elimelech's voice. "Come closer, please."

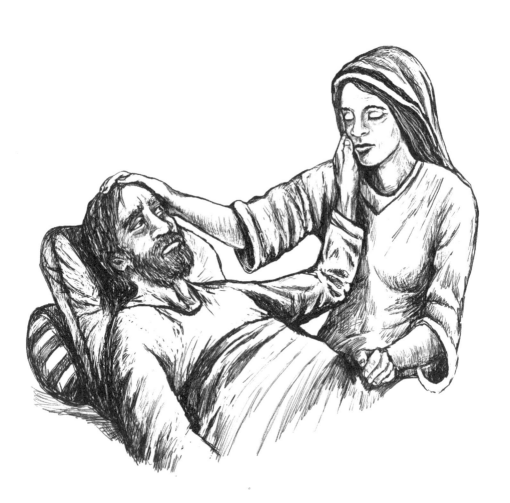

Chapter 6

HE STAYED TOO LONG

"There is a way that seems right to a man,
but in the end it leads to death"
(Proverbs 14:12).

Time kept marching on. . . . Elimelech worked long, hard hours, but somehow the joy of providing for his family had diminished. He often seemed distracted and preoccupied.

"Elimelech, I often hear you tossing and turning in the night. What is wrong, my husband? I've noticed too that your appetite has decreased. You just don't look well to me."

"Oh, don't fuss over me, Naomi. I am the same man I've always been."

But he was not the same man as always. He was having sleepless nights and dreaming bad dreams. In his dreams, he could hear the voice of Boaz calling out to him: *Please don't tarry too long in Moab.*

Had he stayed too long? He thought he knew what was best for his family and himself. Was it so wrong to want to provide for them? In his heart, he knew the answer to his own question. God had promised to meet their needs. Why couldn't he have listened to Naomi and trusted Him to do so? There was a deep hunger in his heart for the way things used to be. He felt a sudden tightness in his chest.

"Naomi! Naomi! Wake up. I can't breathe. Open the door. I need air."

Naomi jumped to her feet. "Try to stay calm. Let me call the boys. They can help get you outside in fresh air. Mahlon, Kilion, come quickly! Your father needs you!"

Mahlon rushed into the room. "What should I do? Should I go for help?"

"I don't know," Naomi answered.

Elimelech spoke between bouts of pain. "No, I don't want a pagan healer. I'll be alright. You boys carry on with the workload until I get better."

But he didn't get better. He continued to grow weaker and weaker. Fear and gloom descended upon their household. Naomi felt so helpless. She remembered God's power and His sovereignty and offered up prayers as she sat by her husband's bedside day and night.

"Naomi!" There was panic in Elimelech's voice. "Come closer, please."

"Yes, my husband." She moved closer. "I'm right here beside you."

"I hunger."

"I have lamb stew for you, my dear," she said with trembling lips.

"No," Elimelech replied in a raspy voice. "No stew . . . bread . . . I hunger for the House of Bread—Bethlehem."

"You want to go back to Bethlehem?"

"Yes, but too late . . . I've stayed . . . too long in Moab." He tried to raise himself up, but his head fell back on the pillow. He reached up and caressed her face with a shaky hand. "I'm sorry, Naomi. May God forgive me."

Chapter 7

A LONELY GRAVE IN MOAB

*"Now Elimelech, Naomi's husband, died, and she
was left with her two sons"* (Ruth 1:3).

Gone—Elimelech was gone! His sojourn was over, but he wouldn't be going home. He was laid to rest next to Shadow . . . on foreign soil . . . pagan soil. The day she buried her husband was the darkest day of Naomi's life.

They had shared so much, the good and the bad. Naomi felt like her heart had been ripped out. And who was there to comfort her?

"Do prayers not count for anything?" she asked God. "What is a widow with two sons supposed to do in a land among strangers?"

If only she could talk to Liora. A woman needs a woman to laugh with, to cry with, and to pray with . . . Liora would understand.

From a heart overflowing with grief, Naomi cried silent tears. *I will lift up my eyes to the hills—where does my help come from? My help comes from the Lord, the Maker of heaven and earth. Help is what I need, Lord. Your help. I can't make it without You.*

From her bedroom, Naomi heard a knock on the door. "Hello Ruth, hello Orpah," she heard Mahlon say.

"We have come to pay our respects," a kind voice said. "We bring sympathy and food from others in our community, lamb stew for your mother. Perhaps it will make her feel better."

"Thank you, Ruth."

Naomi called to her son. "You may invite Ruth and Orpah to come inside, Mahlon."

Ruth stepped into the room and walked over to Naomi and gave her a warm hug. Naomi felt a special connection in her touch. Orpah peeked through the doorway, then shyly stepped in and gave Naomi a gentle pat on her shoulder.

Naomi was moved by the compassion in the eyes of her sons' friends. "May God bless you for your kindness, ladies. Please express my gratitude to your family and friends."

Naomi had asked God for help. She had not expected it to be through the comfort found in the kindness of these Moabite girls. She didn't know what to make of it. *What was God up to?*

Surely His ways are not our ways; His thoughts are not our thoughts.

Chapter 8

NO BOUNDARIES ON LOVE

*"They married Moabite women, one named
Orpah and the other Ruth"* (Ruth 1:4).

T he days and nights were long. Naomi felt
Elimelech's presence everywhere she went.
In her imagination, she could see him bending
over the potter's wheel or see his head bowed to bless
their food.

Naomi had heard from others that "time heals."
But time crept by slowly . . . like the juice of a lemon
that has been squeezed too much.

Mahlon and Kilion seemed to be in their own
little world. They honored and respected Naomi, but
Elimelech as their father had held ultimate authority.
They no longer had a father to look to for advice or
comfort. She worried about their spiritual lives. Would

they remember the things they had been taught about their faith and heritage? The void in their lives was obvious. How could she be both father and mother to her sons?

Her only outlet for her aching heart was working in her garden. When she saw the seeds she planted springing into life, a song of hope arose within her breast.

One sunny day while digging in the soil, Naomi looked up to see Kilion and Mahlon approaching. They seemed a bit uncomfortable.

"Hello, my sons. You're home early. This is a nice surprise."

"Mother, if you have time, we need to talk with you about something important," Mahlon said.

"Of course, my sons. You have all my attention. What is this important matter you wish to speak of?"

Mahlon squirmed. "We wish to get married."

"Married! To the Moabite girls?"

"Yes, of course. We wish to marry Ruth and Orpah."

"But Mah—"

"But *what*, Mother? It's not like we are back in Judah where Israelite women are plentiful. Besides, we love Ruth and Orpah. If you see fit, we would like to live here with you until we can establish homes of our own. Our wives can help with the household chores. It's evident you are lonely without Father. You might come to enjoy their company."

For once in her life, Naomi was speechless. What she had feared most had come true. Her beloved sons were marrying Moabite women, and there was nothing she could do or say that would change things.

Naomi measured her words carefully before she responded. "My sons, you are grown men, free to make your own decisions and learn your own lessons, albeit the hard way. Life experiences have taught me that the ultimate result of our decisions is in the hands of Jehovah God."

With that said, she made a commitment in her heart to live in peace and harmony with Orpah and Ruth and to let God take care of the rest.

The home she now shared with Kilion and Mahlon would become home to their wives also.

Naomi knew her chances of getting back to Bethlehem were growing slimmer each day. *Dear God, please grant me the serenity to accept the things I cannot change, the courage to change the things I can, and the wisdom to know the difference. . . .*

Mahlon and Kilion married the girls from Moab. Ruth and Orpah treated Naomi with courtesy and respect. As she opened her heart to them, she found them opening their hearts to her. They spent many hours together, sewing, making meals, and tending the garden.

They soon became the daughters she never had. *Who knows*, Naomi thought, *maybe someday Ruth and Orpah will bless me with a grandchild. What a joy that would be.*

"My dear wife, you know nothing about making pottery or running a business."

Chapter 9

MORE VISITS
FROM THE
DEATH ANGEL

*"After they had lived there about ten years, both Mahlon and
Kilion also died, and Naomi was left without her two sons
and her husband"* (Ruth 1:4-5).

R uth and Orpah worked hard, eager to please
their husbands who had now taken over the
pottery business. Elimelech had trained them
well. Their business had grown after moving it to the
town square.

Ruth had noticed a difference in Mahlon's energy
level and his eating habits. Her growing concern for
his well-being was plain to see. Her father-in-law had
experienced some of the same symptoms. She tried to
shake off her fear. *Surely Mahlon is too young to die.*

That evening while preparing their meal, Ruth turned to Mother Naomi. "What do you think of me helping Mahlon in the pottery shop? You and Orpah can handle things here, can't you?"

"Of course we can, Ruth, but that is a decision you and Mahlon must make together." The look of concern in Naomi's eyes did not escape Ruth.

"And what decision is that, Mother?"

"Oh hello, Mahlon. I didn't hear you come in. I'll leave it to your wife to answer that question."

Naomi left the room.

"Hello, Mahlon. You're home early, my husband. I was speaking with your mother about my desire to help you and Kilion in the pottery shop. You both have to work such long, hard hours since your father passed. I'd like to lift your load a bit. Mother Naomi and Orpah can carry on here."

"My dear wife, you know nothing about making pottery or running a business."

"But I can *learn*."

"The pottery workplace can be a dangerous place, Ruth. For one thing, it takes special skill to mix the clay just right, or the results could be a lot of broken pottery or even an explosion."

"But . . ."

"But nothing! I will not hear of it. A woman's place is in the home, taking care of her husband and raising children."

"We *have* no children!"

"Well, maybe you should start *thinking* about that! I wish for sons to carry on the family name!"

Speaking in a softer tone, Mahlon handed Ruth a little cup the size a child would drink from. "I made this just today. Let it be a reminder to you, my wife."

Ruth hated to deny Mahlon the joy of having children. It was true that all Hebrew men wanted sons. But she couldn't bear the thought of the possibility of her child being offered as a sacrifice to appease the Moabite god Chemosh. She had witnessed this herself. The memory was forever etched in her mind.

No, not yet.

Some weeks later, the death angel came once again to visit Elimelech's household. Mahlon, a beloved son and husband, died in the night in the arms of Ruth, his Moabite wife.

In their brokenness, Naomi and Ruth reached out to each other, and God sustained them. Ruth began to spend more and more time with Naomi. Although grieving too, Naomi listened and offered Ruth wisdom and support. Their loss created a special bond between them.

Ruth often questioned Naomi about Mahlon's early childhood back in Bethlehem-Judah. She seemed not to be able to hear enough about his Hebrew heritage and about this Jehovah God to whom they offered prayers.

Ruth was feeling restless. There were so many unanswered questions bouncing around in her head. She picked up a shawl and carried it into the sitting room to mend. Naomi and Orpah soon joined her. *Could this be a good time to air her thoughts?* She laid her mending down and looked toward Naomi.

"Mother, you are different from most women I know. You are a woman of strength, compassion, and integrity. Your faith in your God is very obvious. In spite of much sorrow and disappointment in your life, I still hear you singing to this God of yours. Sometimes I hear you praying to Him like you know Him personally. How can this be?"

Naomi was silent for a moment. "My dear Ruth, if I am different, it is because of the grace and mercy of a Holy God. It all goes back to Yahweh, Jehovah God. It started many years ago with Abraham, the father of the nation of Israel. God made a covenant with our people. He promised that He would be our God and we would be His people if we would trust Him and worship Him only.

"I'm sorry to say, we have failed to honor Him as a nation. And I must confess . . . I too have failed at times as a mother and wife and friend. But one thing I know to be true; God will not fail to keep His promises. He is the one true God. All other gods are false gods. They do not deserve to be worshiped."

Ruth drew in a slow breath. "So it is true then, what Mahlon said."

"And what is that, my dear?"

"He said that from the beginning of time, your God had a special plan and purpose for His people. Mahlon said His plan is good and not evil like our god Chemosh, who sometimes demands human sacrifices, even of a child."

"Yes, it is true. God has always had a plan and a purpose for His people, and it is a good one, for He is a good God. If need be, He would give His life to save *us* just as Shadow gave his life to save Kilion from a poisonous snake."

Orpah had been listening intently. She frowned. "But we are Gentiles, Mother. Where does that leave us in this plan of your God?"

"It leaves you in the hands of an Almighty God who has all the answers, Orpah. I am not the judge. We only have to look around to see that we live in a fallen world. Sometimes we mess it up, and sometimes others mess it up. But in spite of the evil around us, God offers us a hope and a future. Don't ever forget that, my daughters. We may not understand it all, but we can trust Him. He can see farther down the road than we."

"Tell me, Mother, how can I get to know this Jehovah God—this Yahweh?" Ruth asked.

Naomi's face lit up. "Keep your ears and eyes open to the truth, Daughter. He will find a way to reveal Himself to you if you seek Him with your whole heart."

"What about this *Promised One*?" Orpah asked.

Naomi looked toward the heavens. "Someday," she said, "the Anointed One, the Promised One, will come and make all things right. Every Hebrew man and every Hebrew woman dreams of becoming the father or mother of this promised Redeemer. In the meantime, our people continue to wait. God always keeps His promises. He'll keep this one in the fullness of time. He is never too early or too late. He is always right on time . . . His time."

Ruth found herself longing to know more.

"Oh, Ruth, Orpah, it blesses my heart to know that Mahlon and Kilion didn't forget at least *some* of our teachings." Naomi stood. "Come now, daughters, walk with me to the pottery shop. I feel the need to see the face of my son."

The three women meandered toward the pottery shop to visit with Kilion. As they approached the town square, a booming noise made them stop in their tracks. They looked at each other. *What could it be? What was going on?*

"Stand back!" A man yelled. "We're coming through! This man is badly hurt." People were running to and fro.

Orpah started running toward the pottery shop. The sound of her screams echoed back to Ruth and Naomi.

Fear paralyzed Naomi.

"Oh no, God! Please, don't let it be Kilion!" she cried. "I've already lost one son. He's all I have."

Ruth reached out and caught Naomi before she slumped to the ground.

Hours later, Naomi awoke in her own bed. For a moment, she was back in Bethlehem, watching Mahlon and Kilion play with Shadow. The fog lifted. Reality set in when she heard the heart-wrenching sobs of Ruth and the angry words of Orpah.

"Why? Why? He was too young to die. Where was Naomi's God today?"

Naomi remained silent for she had no answer. She had no words with which to comfort her daughter-in-law. Her own mind was also filled with *"whys?"*

Chapter 10
A RUMOR OF BREAD

"When she heard in Moab that the Lord had come to the aid of his people by providing food for them" (Ruth 1:6).

In the lonely days ahead, Naomi's raw emotions flip-flopped from denial to guilt—from depression to anger. Why had Elimelech not listened when she begged him not to move to Moab? She often redirected her anger toward herself.

Should she have protested more? Perhaps Elimelech would have changed his mind and stayed in Bethlehem if she had been more persistent. Now they were all gone. She was a lonely, broken woman without a song to sing.

Ruth and Orpah missed the old Naomi. Their grief was compounded by her grief. But she was lost in a dark world all her own.

Orpah and Ruth sat talking in the home that was now filled with so many empty places. Ruth sighed deeply. "How I miss Mother Naomi's sweet smile and her unexpected laughter. I miss hearing her sing while she kneads dough and works in her garden."

"I know what you mean, Ruth," Orpah responded. "She was once a strong woman who faced life with courage and determination. It is not like her to be so weak and bitter. It seems she has lost all interest in life. Every attempt to comfort her has failed."

"We can identify with her pain of losing a husband, Orpah. But we can't identify with her pain of losing her sons also. I can think of no greater loss."

"You are right, of course, but surely there is something we can do."

"Let's try again," Ruth said.

They walked into Naomi's room and found her huddled up in a chair in the corner.

"Mother, come to the market with us today," Ruth said. "The fresh air will be good for you."

"How do you know what will be good for me? I'm an old woman with no husband, no children, and no grandchildren. Tell me, what do I have to live for? I wish I had died instead of my sons."

"Well, it is not so easy for Ruth and me either," Orpah retorted. "We have lost the loves of our lives."

"Mother, I have some news that might interest you," Ruth said. "I saw a man from Bethlehem in town yesterday. He came from Judah with a caravan. He said it is raining in Bethlehem. The famine is over, and there is food in abundance."

Naomi jumped up quickly and hurried to Ruth. "Are you sure? He said it is raining? I must find him. When I left Bethlehem, it was a dry and thirsty land. If it is true that God is pouring out His blessings on my people and my homeland again . . . then it is time for me to return home."

"Home? This is your home, Mother," Orpah said. "It *has* been for many years."

"No, this was Elimelech and Mahlon and Kilion's home, but not mine. Home is where your heart is. My heart has always been in Bethlehem. This was just a sojourn. I must return to the God of my fathers."

"But Mother," Orpah said. "How will you get there? No offense meant, but you are much older than when you came here."

"I'll get there the same way my people got to the land of Canaan . . . by putting one foot in front of the other. Don't worry about me. I'll be gone a while. I'm not as fast on my feet as I once was."

"Let me go with you, Mother," Ruth said. "I will recognize the man if we see him."

"No. This is something I must do on my own. Now try to have a good day, my daughters. I shall return before dark."

Ruth followed her to the door and watched her walk away.

With mixed emotions, she turned back to Orpah. "Did you see the excitement in Mother Naomi's eyes? It has been a long time since I have seen any life there. Do you suppose she meant it when she said she was going to return to Bethlehem?"

"I feel sure she meant it," Orpah said, shrugging her shoulders. "She has never stopped talking about her homeland *and* her God."

"You're right. I guess we should not be surprised at Mother Naomi's decision. But Orpah, we can't let her travel alone. It is not safe."

"Perhaps she can join a caravan going that way."

"But still, she would have to camp at night with strangers," Ruth said. "Can you imagine the mother of our dear husbands doing that? Most likely, some of the people in the caravan would not respect a woman traveling alone. If she goes through with her plan, I feel I must go with her. It is the right thing to do. Besides, she is the only connection we have with Mahlon and Kilion."

"Ruth, are you serious? Yes, I can see that you are. There's more to it than just being with our husbands' mother, isn't there? I've observed how you cling to every word Mother Naomi utters about this Jehovah God—this Yahweh, she calls Him. Could this be your *real* reason for going to Bethlehem with Naomi?"

"I must confess; you are partly right. I can't explain it, but there is a longing in my heart. Something down deep in my spirit makes me yearn to know this God of Naomi's, to know Him in the way that she knows Him. Perhaps in Bethlehem, I might find this God who pursues me day and night."

"I must admit, He sounds like a more loving God than some of ours," Orpah said. "But Ruth, right or wrong, this is our home and our people. I love Naomi like a mother, but I like it here. The fear of the unknown would prevent me from making such a choice, I believe."

"Well, maybe we won't have to. Perhaps Mother Naomi will change her mind."

"Don't count on it, Ruth. I've heard it said that blood is thicker than water."

"Oh, Daughter! I'm afraid you don't know what you're getting yourself into, but I see it is useless to argue."

Chapter 11

HOMEWARD BOUND

"Naomi and her daughters-in-law prepared to return home from there" (Ruth 1:6).

Naomi returned home before Orpah and Ruth had time to start worrying.

"Hello, my daughters! Remember what you said about rain? I found the man in charge of the caravan at the waterhole, watering his animals. It is indeed raining in Bethlehem. He will be leaving in three days. That gives me just enough time to take care of business and pack a few belongings."

"Mother, are you sure this is what you want to do?" Ruth asked.

"I find it hard to believe you would leave after all these years," Orpah said.

"My mind is made up," she said. "I've been dreaming about going home for years. I have made arrangements to join a caravan going near Bethlehem. Now I must get some rest. The journey will not be an easy one. Good night, my daughters, and may God give you sweet rest."

Naomi left the girls standing, looking at each other. She went to her room and lay down on her pallet but remained awake. She and Elimelech had always planned to go back home to Bethlehem, and now was the time. True, she was old now and alone. Could she make the trip back? Could she bear to leave her husband and sons buried beneath the soil in a heathen nation? Would her family and friends even know her? So many questions . . .

And what about Ruth and Orpah? She loved them as if they were her own daughters. Oh, how she would miss them! But go, she must. She refused to live out the rest of her life in Moab. It was a forbidden place, an unhappy place.

She had left Bethlehem looking back. She would leave Moab looking forward—to what, she didn't know. *I'll just take one day at a time*, she decided. *After all, that's how we're supposed to live. Just one day at a time.*

"Oh, Bethlehem," she whispered, "how I long to see your green pastures and walk on your soil once again. . . ." With that picture in her mind, a special kind of peace descended upon her, and she drifted off to sleep.

Dawn came early. Bags were packed. Naomi called Orpah and Ruth to her side.

"Dear daughters, it is time for me to say goodbye. It grieves me so to leave you, but go I must—echoes from the past pull me back. I want to die in my own homeland."

"It is not goodbye, Mother. We are going with you," Ruth said.

"What do you mean, going with me? Are you serious? Then hurry, we must be on our way. The caravan leaves soon."

Naomi was energized by the thought of seeing the House of Bread again. The girls could hardly keep up with her pace. As they entered the campground of the caravan, Naomi stopped abruptly.

"Ruth, Orpah, stop! What could I have been thinking? You cannot come with me. I won't allow it. You must turn around and go back to the houses of your mothers and fathers."

"But we want to come with you. Please don't send us back," Ruth pleaded.

"No, you must stay here. I was using my heart when I allowed you to come with me—now I must use my head. You know nothing of living in a foreign land among strangers. There is no sickness like homesickness. It will end up squeezing the very life out of you."

"But Mother Naomi, we will miss you greatly," Orpah said.

"Dear daughters, you have dealt kindly toward me and were loving wives to my dear sons. I will carry you in my heart forever and cherish every moment we've had together, but it would not be fair to you. You are young. Go back to your own mothers and fathers and find husbands. Marry and have children. I have no more sons to offer you. Go *now*!"

The sounds of braying donkeys, bleating goats, and the shouts of people filled the air. The caravan began moving out. Naomi turned and kissed Orpah and Ruth goodbye. Their tears mingled together as they clung to each other.

"Mother, it hurts to say goodbye, but I think it is best that I stay here with my own people," Orpah said. "Please understand. I won't soon forget the things you taught me about living and loving and about your God."

"Goodbye, my dear Orpah. My heart aches from knowing I may never see you again, but I understand. I don't fault you for not leaving your own people and going into an unknown country. I couldn't guarantee a good life for you and Ruth in Bethlehem. I don't know what I will find when I return. I've been away so long. I'm sure many changes have occurred."

After one last embrace, Orpah turned and walked away, tears streaming down her face.

Naomi looked at Ruth. "Your sister-in-law is going back to live with her own people and her gods. Go with her."

Ruth moved closer to Naomi as the caravan started to move out.

"Ruth, did you hear me?" Naomi pushed her away. "Go *now*! I insist."

"No. Please don't force me to leave you. Please don't make me go back. Where you go, *I* will go, and where you live, *I* will live. Your people will be *my* people. I ask for nothing more."

Naomi couldn't believe what her ears had heard. "But Ruth, you—"

Ruth clutched Naomi's arm. "Don't you understand, Mother? *Your God is my God.* Where you die, I shall die, and that's where I will be buried, so help me God—not even *death itself* is going to come between us!"

"Oh Daughter! I'm afraid you don't know what you're getting yourself into, but I see it is useless to argue. Come what may, we will make this journey together." She glanced at the retreating caravan then back to Ruth. "We must hurry now, or we will be left behind."

The journey back to Bethlehem was a long and treacherous one over rocky terrain. Ruth prayed they would have enough food and water to last to the journey's end. She had packed some dried fruit, wheat cakes, and lamb jerky. Hopefully the sheepskin water canteens could be refilled when they stopped to camp for the night.

Ruth and Naomi each carried a large bag. Each bag held a blanket, an extra pair of sandals, a tunic, and a shawl. The smaller bags they carried had mysterious bulges. Neither woman questioned the other. Even family members had a right to their privacy, they believed.

The conversation was plentiful on their journey. Naomi painted a word picture of the little town of Bethlehem while keeping a cautious eye on the others in the caravan. When she started to describe her home and the way it looked when they left Bethlehem, unexpected anger at Elimelech boiled up inside her.

Naomi reached for Ruth's arm. "What have I gotten you into, Daughter? I'm returning to my homeland empty-handed except for the clothes on my back . . . so little to show for years of love and laughter . . . and tears."

Ruth could see that the journey home was a bittersweet experience for Naomi. She reached over and gave her a hug. After a long pause, Naomi spoke again.

"When Elimelech decided to go to Moab, he mortgaged our land. It's possible he mortgaged our home too. I won't know until we get to Bethlehem. The reality is, we may not have a place to lay our heads when we get there."

Ruth stopped walking. "Look at me, Mother. You worry too much. We'll face this together when the time comes. It will be alright."

Naomi tried to keep pace with the others, but after hours of weary travel, she stumbled and fell. Ruth gently helped her rise to a standing position.

One of the caravan drivers stopped beside them. "Hey, you with the old woman! Climb up into my wagon. Rest will do you both good."

Naomi spoke softly to Ruth. "My daughter, I may be old, but I'm not blind. It is not my well-being that he is concerned about. It's you he wants to sit beside. Be careful; your beauty would captivate any man."

"Oh, Mother, how you do go on," Ruth said with a chuckle. "I can take care of myself. I can tell that you are growing weary. Let's accept his offer."

"Alright, but you watch out for him!"

It was good to know that Naomi still had a spark of fire in her. The special treatment shown to them, however, was frowned upon by the Hebrews returning to Bethlehem from their buying trip to Moab. What's an old Hebrew woman doing with a young Moabite maiden, they must wonder? Surely she is not taking her to the land of the Israelites.

If Ruth noticed the stares or heard the whispers, she did not let on.

Naomi grew quiet as they sat in the wagon, her eyes troubled.

Ruth glanced her way. "Mother, I understand your concern for me. I beg of you, please don't worry about me. You left your homeland and moved to a foreign land. You not only survived but thrived. God willing, I will do the same. I am trusting Jehovah God to take care of us."

It was true. Naomi was concerned. What would her friends and family have to say about her returning with a Moabite daughter-in-law? Would they accept Ruth for the special person she was, or would they taunt her or perhaps ostracize her?

As the caravan moved closer to Bethlehem, Naomi saw that God indeed had brought life-giving nourishment to her beloved homeland. The pastures were green. The lakes had water in them once again. The trees were lush with fruit. The bitterness in her heart could not override her joy. She clapped her hands when she saw the little village of Bethlehem nestled on the hillside. Home at last! She looked at Ruth and saw her bewilderment.

Ruth spoke in a voice full of awe. "Mother, I'd like to celebrate your joy, but right now it is just too much for me to take in . . . being on the same soil that Mahlon walked on and played on . . . I will ponder on this later."

"Don't call me Naomi; call me Mara.
Life has dealt me a bitter blow."

Chapter 12
CALL ME BITTER

' "Don't call me Naomi," she told them. "Call me Mara,
because the Almighty has made my life very bitter.
I went away full, but the Lord has brought me back empty"'
(Ruth 1:20-21).

The driver of the wagon stopped outside the gates of the town square. Ruth disembarked first, then helped Naomi down from the wagon. With their heads held high, hand-in-hand, they walked down the road into the little town of Bethlehem.

"Look, Mother," Ruth said. "It seems the whole town is buzzing with activity. I didn't expect Bethlehem to be such a busy place. People are looking our way. Do you recognize anyone?"

"Yes, yes, I do. Is this a welcoming committee?" Naomi spoke with surprise. "There is my best friend

Liora with her husband Adley! My, my, she has aged. Surely I don't look *that* old. Look! That must be Jaden and Nava with them. I suppose they are married with families of their own by now."

Liora ran to Naomi with her arms open wide. She turned to the crowd that had gathered. "Look, everyone. Here is our dear, sweet Naomi!"

Naomi's stomach churned. Did they not know what had happened to her? She crossed her arms. "Don't call me Naomi; call me Mara. Life has dealt me a bitter blow. My life was full when I left here, but God has brought me back empty. Loss of my loved ones has ruined me. Why would you call me Naomi, a name that means pleasant and sweet? God certainly doesn't. I have nothing but the clothes on my back."

"Naomi dear, the news of your misfortune traveled back here to Bethlehem. You have suffered much. I'm so sorry for your losses. We have grieved with you and for you. Thank God you are now back with your own people who love you."

Naomi winced at Liora's words. *Your own people.* She saw Ruth take a step back. Was this an indication of how things would be for Ruth? She could imagine how the remark made her feel. Would she always be considered an outsider?

Naomi reached back and pulled Ruth up beside her. "Liora, this is my dear daughter-in-law, Ruth. I love her like a daughter. She is as beautiful inside as she is outside. I know you will love her when you get to know her."

"I'm sure I will," Liora said. "Thank you, Ruth, for looking out for my friend. Naomi, is there anything Adley and I can do to help? Where will you be staying? You are welcome at our house. We have a lot to catch up on. I'll fix a nice meal, and you can spend the night if you wish. I've missed you so much."

"Thank you, dear friend. We'll go to your house first. A cool drink of water and a little rest will be sufficient for now." She looked at Adley. "After we rest a bit, I want to check out our old home place. If it isn't occupied by someone, perhaps we can clean it up and live there."

Adley shuffled his feet. "The house is still standing, Naomi, but I'm sorry to tell you that the land has fallen into the hands of another."

"I was expecting that it would be so, Adley. We were away from our obligations for a long time."

After a short detour to Liora's house, Naomi and Ruth were ready to move on.

"Thank you, friends. We'll be back later. It's so good to be home."

"Mother," Ruth said, "I feel like I have friends in Nava and Jaden."

"I prayed it would be so, my child."

With her body aching, Naomi continued through the town with Ruth by her side. They made their way up a rocky path to a place that Naomi hardly recognized. Time had indeed changed the landscape of the place she once called home. She glanced toward the little garden place, the place she had escaped to for solace after she had learned of Elimelech's plan to move to Moab. The place where she had poured her heart out to Liora was now a garden of weeds.

A broken trellis leaned against a crumbling wall. "See that broken trellis, Ruth? It used to be ablaze with beautiful roses. Look at it now. It describes me," she said with a trembling voice. "It takes light to make a flower grow. My light went out when my husband and sons died."

Suddenly she remembered Liora's words like it was yesterday: *Maybe God, in His time and in His providence, will bring something good from this sojourn in Moab.*

Naomi whispered, "Please, Lord, let it be so. I'm waiting, Lord. Yes, You gave me Ruth, and I am grateful. I still find it hard to believe that she would sacrifice her youth to come here to live with an old worn out mother-in-law. But I'm afraid, Lord. Where will we live? What will we live on?"

Naomi stepped up onto the crumbling porch and walked into a room filled with cobwebs and dust.

Memories, some as soft as a mother's lap, others as painful as an open wound came crashing in . . . faces she used to see, voices she used to hear, little hands she used to hold. Was that a dog barking . . . Shadow? It was so surreal. She put her head in her hands as sobs shook her frail frame. Tears she had bottled up since the death of her dear husband and precious sons spilled over onto the dirty floor like water from a broken cistern.

With the tears, she felt the coldness around her heart begin to melt. She released her bitterness. Her spirit was renewed. A new sense of strength and purpose arose within her heart and spirit.

Ruth didn't enter the house with Naomi. She sat down on the crumbling doorstep and waited. What a contrast to the comfortable home she had lived in back in Moab. For the first time, she understood what Naomi was talking about when she had said: "There is no sickness like homesickness."

"God, if You are real, and I believe You are, hear my prayer for strength and safety and bread for our table," she prayed aloud.

Such a simple prayer was Ruth's, coming from an aching heart filled with uneasiness. She felt not only her own pain but the pain of her dear mother-in-law. *Does God really put our tears in a bottle as Naomi once said? That bottle must be full to overflowing.*

There, in the midst of what seemed like a sacred moment, Ruth sensed an unexplainable presence and experienced peace that passed understanding.

Naomi found Ruth, head bowed in prayer, sitting on the steps where she had left her. Ruth stood up.

"Mother Naomi, death has broken our hearts, but we can't allow it to break our spirits. We have to pick up the pieces of our lives and move forward."

"You are right, Daughter. The Lord gives and the Lord takes away; may the name of the Lord be praised. I'll enlist the help of Jaden and Nava. We'll make this place livable again, I promise you."

Chapter 13

BRINGING IN THE SHEAVES

*"As it turned out, she found herself working in a field
belonging to Boaz, who was from the clan of Elimelech"*
(Ruth 2:3).

Life settled in for Ruth and Naomi. With the help of Nava and Jaden, the house was made livable. For the next few weeks, old friends and relatives generously shared from the bounty God had provided them: grain, fruit, milk, and honey. Some came by out of curiosity. They wanted to see the Moabite daughter-in-law. Others came because they had a sympathetic heart toward Naomi for all she had been through.

Ruth knew, however, that this could not go on forever. She was appreciative, but she was not content with what she interpreted as "charity." She was determined to find a way to provide for them.

While working with Naomi in the little garden they had planted, Ruth presented a solution to her.

"Mother, when I went to the village well today, I heard that in your culture the landowners are required to leave the corners of the field for the poor, especially the widows, to glean in."

"You heard right, Daughter."

"It is barley harvesting time. Many are going into the fields and picking up the leftover grain. I too can do that. It is not good to depend on others to do for us what we can do for ourselves. Look at me. I'm young and strong. I ask your permission to glean among the sheaves."

Naomi stopped working and took a deep breath. "Dear daughter, I hate that it has come to this, but it seems our only solution for now. But please be careful. All Hebrew men are not gentlemen. There are those who might harm you."

"Don't go fretting yourself, Mother. Surely I can find a harvester who will treat me kindly. I'm certainly not interested in any of those flirtatious men, and I can't see any godly ones wanting to be seen with a Moabitess."

"Don't put yourself down. You have already gained the respect of many people. Mahlon saw the goodness in you, or he would not have chosen you. You are young. Someday your thoughts will turn again to love. A godly love is a beautiful thing, Ruth. That's my desire for you."

"It would take someone very special to win my heart again. I don't expect that to happen, Mother."

Naomi pointed toward the flower garden. "I didn't expect that Rose of Sharon to ever bloom again either, but look at it."

"Let's have no more talk about men today, Mother. We should go in. I must rise early in the morning to go into the fields."

Ruth slept fitfully, her thoughts troubled. She rehashed Naomi's words in her mind. *Would it be possible to someday find love again in this foreign land among Mahlon's people and their God? Their God? No—My God. What a comforting thought that was.*

As she drifted off, unspoken words hung in the air like fluffy clouds in the sky. *To my husband-to-be; whoever you are and wherever you are—I need you tonight. I need you to listen to my heart, to see my need for a godly love but also for a passionate love. I want to be able to look into your eyes and just see the two of us and our love for each other. I want a love built on trust, respect, and a love that's unique.*

I would never want to betray you or dishonor you in any way. I want to give of myself, share the good and bad, the joys and sorrows, the hopes and dreams. I want to be able to speak of spiritual things, pray together, and laugh together. I want a family and a child to love.

Then Ruth slept.

Morning came too soon. Time waits for no one, and the fields were ripe for harvesting. A large number of women were already gathering barley for their daily bread.

"Stay close to the other women," Naomi had said. Ruth understood why now. When she attempted to glean in the first field, someone called her a bad name and threw a handful of grain in her face. She moved on to another field and started gleaning.

The sun was hot on her back. Perspiration dripped from her nose. So this was what the poor of Bethlehem did to survive. . . . *I can do this. I can do this. Pride is not an issue when you're hungry.*

The sound of a cheerful male voice caught Ruth's attention. She looked up and saw a man in proper riding attire on a white stallion. *This man must be someone important.*

"Good morning. The Lord be with you," the man said to the harvesters.

"The Lord bless you also," the harvesters answered respectfully.

For just a minute, the rider looked in Ruth's direction. She went back to gleaning, but the wind blew their remarks toward her. She wiped the sweat from her face as the stranger continued in conversation with the foreman.

"Zachary, who is that young woman? I haven't seen her here before."

Ruth looked at the stranger and shivered. *Does he know I'm a Moabite? Will he ask me to leave?*

The foreman pointed toward the woman. "She is the foreigner, Boaz, the one who came back with Naomi from Moab. She showed up here and asked to glean and gather among the sheaves behind the harvesters. She has worked steadily from morning till now, except for a short rest in the shelter."

"So this is Mahlon's widow from Moab! I heard all about her just today when I returned from my business trip. Her name is Ruth."

Even with a sweaty face, Ruth's beauty was evident to Boaz. He couldn't explain how one glimpse of her made him want to protect her.

Boaz dismounted his stallion and handed the reins to Zachary. Approaching Ruth, he spoke her name quietly. She looked up at him fearfully.

"Don't be afraid, young one. I am Boaz. So you are Naomi's daughter-in-law. I must pay her a visit. I hear she lost everything dear to her. Some are saying she also lost her faith."

Ruth straightened up and looked directly into Boaz's eyes. "I beg to differ, kind sir. She has *not* lost her faith. It is only buried beneath the pain and heartache that has been thrust upon her. Naomi is a special woman with an extraordinary faith."

Boaz was touched by Ruth's quick reaction. "I must say, I admire your loyalty. You are right, of course. I have great respect for Naomi. It is good to see that she has gained a daughter-in-law who loves her so much. I have heard many good things about you."

"Thank you, kind sir."

"Listen to me. Don't go and glean in another field and don't go away from here. Stay here with my servant girls. Watch the field where the men are harvesting and follow along after the girls. I will tell the men not to touch you. Whenever you are thirsty, go and get a drink from the water jars the men have filled."

Ruth fell to her knees. "Oh, sir, why have I found favor in your eyes that you notice me—a foreigner?"

Boaz extended his hand. "Get up from the ground, young daughter. Your humility is admirable, but it is not necessary to bow down to me. There is only one God, and I am not He. I've been told about all you have done for your mother-in-law since the death of your husband—how you left your father and mother and your homeland and came here to live among strangers. May you be richly rewarded by the Lord, the God of Israel, under whose wings you have come to take refuge."

Something in Boaz's voice kindled something inside Ruth that had lain dormant for a long time. Seeing the kindness in his eyes, she felt safe for the first time since arriving in Bethlehem. "I pray I continue to find favor in your eyes, my lord. You have given me comfort and have spoken kindly to me—though I do not have the standing of one of your servant girls.

Excuse me now. I must return to work." As she turned to go, Ruth heard a man's shrill whistle. It seemed to come from the winepress area. Her face flushed with embarrassment.

Boaz walked to where Zachary stood waiting with his horse. "Who was that, Zachary? Get his name and keep an eye on him. I will have none of that young man's foolishness in my field."

Boaz approached Ruth again at mealtime when the harvesters came to the shelter. "Come over here, young lady. Have some bread and dip it in the wine vinegar."

"You are kind, sir. Thank you," she said. A shy smile lit up her face.

"Here. Have some roasted grain," Boaz said as Ruth sat down with the harvesters.

She ate all she wanted and had some left over. As she got up to glean, Boaz quietly gave orders.

"Even if she gathers among the sheaves, don't embarrass her. Rather, pull out some stalks for her from the bundles and leave them for her to pick up. Don't rebuke her. Watch out for her."

Zachary repressed a smile.

Boaz spent more time in the fields than usual that day. He sometimes sat on his horse or beneath a tree near the edge of the field where his faithful steward Zachary and his assistant Gabe watched the gleaners.

"Our master may not realize it yet, but I believe he is smitten by the foreign girl," Zachary remarked.

"Can't say that I blame him, Zachary, but she is a Gentile, you know."

"Boaz wouldn't hold that against her. After all, Rahab was his mother."

"So?"

"I see you haven't heard the story, Gabe. She was once known as Rahab, a Gentile harlot. When the Israelites were ready to move into the land of Canaan, they sent two spies to check things out. Rahab had enough faith to believe that God would give the land to the Israelites, so she hid the Hebrew spies and kept them from being killed. God took note of her because of this heroic act. Her life and that of her family were spared when the invasion occurred. Salmon married her, and they had Boaz. God grafted her into the covenant He made with the Israelites. A better woman you could never find. Boaz wouldn't be the man he is today if it were not for his mother's faith and sacrifice."

Zachary gave Gabe a stern look and added, "We must not let any harm come to Ruth, or we'll both be out of a job."

Boaz was not offended by the conversation he overheard between the two men. It was from his mother that he had learned that God's grace is greater than sin. He knew these men well. He could trust them. But could he trust his own heart to remain untouched by this beautiful young foreigner?

Naomi stood in the doorway, waiting to greet Ruth when she returned from a long, hot day of gleaning in the field. It grieved her to see the tired look on the beautiful face as Ruth handed her the barley.

"How are you, my dear? Did everything go alright in the field?"

"Gleaning is hard work, Mother, but it is a good place to dream. Let me wash up, and then we will talk." Ruth went to the wash basin and found that Naomi had filled it already. She splashed water on her face and rubbed her hands together.

"I have your meal ready," Naomi said.

"Good," Ruth responded as she dried her hands. "I'm hungry."

They sat down, bowed their heads, and thanked God for His provision.

"Well, my daughter, it appears that you had a productive day. Whose field did you glean in? God bless whoever it was that took such good care of you."

Ruth dipped her bread into the warm soup. "His name is Boaz, Mother."

"Boaz? The Lord bless him! He is an honorable man. He has not stopped showing his kindness and respect for the living and the dead. Boaz is a cousin of Elimelech's."

Suddenly a light came on for Naomi. *She had a plan, but the success of it didn't depend on her.*

"Ruth! Boaz is one of our kinsman-redeemers."

"I'm afraid I have much to learn about your Hebrew heritage and culture, Mother. I don't understand this talk about a 'kinsman-redeemer.' "

"I can understand your confusion, my dear," said Naomi. "I'll try to explain this unique relationship with Jehovah God and His covenant people. The faith of our people is a generational faith that started with Abraham. God chose Abraham to be the father of the nation of Israel. He was a mighty man of faith."

"Tell me more," Ruth said as she pushed her bowl away.

"As Elimelech's and Mahlon's heirs, you and I have the right to reclaim the land that Elimelech lost to another. But as you know, I cannot redeem it and neither can you. We haven't the means to do so."

She continued, "A kinsman-redeemer, a close relative, has the opportunity and the obligation to become a guardian who is responsible to protect the inheritance of a deceased family member or members by marrying the relative's widow and raising children in his name. Therefore, the generational name would not be struck from the town records. If you were to marry a kinsman-redeemer, should you have a son, he would carry the name of Mahlon."

"What a strange custom, Mother."

"Oh, Ruth, there may be hope for us yet."

Ruth got up from her chair. "We can't live on hope alone, Mother. Right now, I'll settle for a comfortable place to sleep. Tomorrow will be another long day in the barley field."

Boaz began to look forward to seeing Ruth among the gleaners each day. It was not just her outward beauty, although she was beautiful; it was something more, a connection he really couldn't define. He found himself thinking about her day and night. It thrilled him to the core of his being just to see her shy smile and hear her sweet voice. Just yesterday, he heard her singing while she worked.

How could someone as old as he capture the heart of someone as young and beautiful as Ruth? She could have most any man, those much younger than him. He didn't expect to ever hold her in his arms, only in his heart, yet he found every excuse he could to speak with her.

Boaz started arriving earlier in the field each morning. Feeling a pull on his heartstrings, he walked over to Ruth. "Shalom. What a nice morning. Tell me, how is Naomi faring these days?"

"I'm happy to report that she is eating well and feeling much better, my lord. We have you to thank for that."

"I'm glad to hear that. Is there anything you need? Perhaps I could have some of my workers repair the house before the weather turns colder."

"We are doing quite well, my lord. It's kind of you to offer. I'll pass it on to Naomi."

"If I may, I would like to call you Ruth."

She nodded. For a moment, their eyes locked. When her hand accidentally brushed his, it felt like a holy moment.

Boaz could deny it no longer. He was in love with the beautiful foreigner. Her face was the last thing he saw before going to sleep at night and the first thing he saw upon awakening.

Every time Ruth heard Boaz's voice, her heart beat faster. In her dreams at night, it was the voice of Boaz she heard and not Mahlon's. *Would Boaz be shocked to know how I feel?*

True, he wasn't handsome like Mahlon, but when she heard others speak of the goodness of Yahweh, the face of Boaz came before her—his kindness, his compassion, and his faith in Jehovah God. But they lived in two different worlds. He was a rich landowner.

Who was she but a poor widow from the pagan land of Moab? He was an Israelite, and she was a Gentile. "In Bethlehem, Israelite men marry Israelite women," Naomi had once said to her and Orpah.

Boaz was kind and compassionate to all widows. That's the kind of man he was. No, it could never be. She must force Boaz from her thoughts.

She and Naomi were safe, healthy, and had food on the table. That's what she had prayed for. That had to be enough.

Many weeks later, as the sun set in the west, Ruth returned home, gripped with a loneliness she had not experienced before.

The harvest time was coming to an end. Ruth's aching body could use some rest, but her life would seem so empty without seeing Boaz ride into the field each day. It would be such a long time until the next harvest.

Why, oh why, did I allow my heart to be touched by this man whom I can never know except as an employer?

She felt the weight of the world on her shoulders. *I'm here, Lord. Do You see me?*

"That sounds shameful, Mother.
I'm surprised you would suggest
such a thing."

Chapter 14
A BARLEY ROMANCE

"Ruth approached quietly, uncovered his feet
and lay down" (Ruth 3:7).

As Ruth neared home, she stopped in her tracks. Was that singing she heard? It couldn't be.

Naomi was singing at the top of her voice: *"I will enter His gates with thanksgiving in my heart. I will enter His courts with praise! I will say this is the day that the Lord has made. I will rejoice, for He has made me glad. . . . "*

Was this the same Naomi who had greeted her yesterday? Ruth quickened her pace.

"Mother!" she said as she opened the door. "What has come over you?"

"Nothing, dear. Just exercising my voice." She walked over and gave Ruth a hug. "Child, I've been thinking . . . maybe it's time I should try to find a home for you where you will be well provided for. I'm not getting any younger, you know. It would give me great peace to see you married and settled in a comfortable home, raising children. I long to hold a child of yours in my lap before I pass from this life."

"That would be nice, Mother, but there's not much chance of that happening."

"I hear Boaz has been riding into the barley field more often than usual since you started working among the sheaves," Naomi said with a smile.

Ruth laughed. "Where did you hear that gossip?"

"When I went to the market, I overheard Jaden and Nava talking. Jaden said you couldn't be interested in Boaz. He said Boaz was too old for you. I do believe he has his eye on you for himself."

"Oh, Mother, there you go trying to match-make. And what did Nava have to say?"

Naomi grinned. "She said, 'I'd rather be an old man's darling than a young man's slave.' She has a point you know. Since Boaz is a kinsman of ours, I thought perhaps . . ."

"Mother, you must be dreaming!" Ruth threw her hands up. "Boaz is not interested in *me*. He is sought after by every available woman in all of Bethlehem and beyond. I'm just a foreigner from Moab. I would be the last person he would choose to marry."

"You might be pleasantly surprised, my daughter. Tonight may be your night! Wash and put on your prettiest tunic. Use the perfume in the vase I brought from Moab."

"Perfume?"

"Yes, Elimelech gave it to me for my birthday. Now just do as I say. Boaz and the other men will be winnowing the barley on the threshing floor tonight. Go there, and don't let him know you are there until they get through celebrating the harvest with their food and drinks. When he lies down and goes to sleep, go to where he is lying, uncover his feet, and lie down there."

Ruth brought her hand to her mouth. "That sounds shameful, Mother. I'm surprised you would suggest such a thing. I'm not *that* eager to have a husband."

"You don't understand, Daughter. In our culture this is acceptable. There is nothing sinful about it. You can trust Boaz, for he is an honorable man. When you lie at his feet, this lets him know that you desire to marry him if he so chooses."

Ruth sighed. "I am not comfortable with this plan of yours, Mother, but if you say it is the right thing to do, I will do it—for you. I trust you, and I trust Boaz. But what if Boaz isn't interested in me? What do I do then?"

"You don't do anything, Ruth. Just sit back and watch God work!"

Ruth reluctantly accepted her mother-in-law's counsel. She put on her second-best tunic. Somehow, it didn't seem appropriate to wear the one she had worn when she had married Mahlon. She added a fringed shawl.

"You look beautiful," Naomi said. She kissed Ruth on her cheek. "May God go with you, my daughter," she whispered.

Ruth left the house, walking slowly. She was not eager to follow Naomi's suggestion. She kept watching to her left and to her right. Her mind went back to the whistle she'd heard on the first day of gleaning in the barley field.

Did she hear movement? Was that a shadow at the edge of the field?

With a sigh of relief, she saw that it was Jaden. Maybe Naomi was right about him after all. When she glanced his way, he quickly turned and disappeared. She relaxed. She had nothing to fear from Jaden. She had found him to be trustworthy. *I must be cautious lest I am seen by someone who would think badly of me.*

She finally reached the threshing area. Standing in a secluded place, she saw that the eating and drinking was winding down. She felt like running away, but she knew she must follow Naomi's instructions as closely as possible. She had come to trust Boaz without reservation because he trusted Jehovah God, the God Naomi trusted and the One she had come to trust. She watched as Boaz went over to lie down alone at the far end of the grain pile.

When he was sleeping soundly, Ruth crept down to the place where Boaz lay. She uncovered his feet and lay down. She hardly dared breathe. Time dragged on.

In the middle of the night, Boaz was startled when he turned over and found a woman lying at his feet. "Who are you?" he demanded.

"I am Ruth, your servant. Please, my lord, take me under your protective wing and spread your garment over me. You are Mahlon's close relative, you know. In the circle of covenant redeemers, you have the right to marry me."

Boaz sat up quickly. Ruth's nearness took his breath away, but he knew he must keep his head on straight. For Ruth, this was most likely just a business arrangement suggested by Naomi.

"The Lord bless you, my dear! What a splendid expression of love. You have not run after younger men, whether rich or poor, though you could have had your pick, I'm sure. Now don't be afraid. I will do for you all that you ask."

Ruth could hardly believe what she was hearing. "But my lord, may I remind you that I am a Moabitess and unworthy of your favor?"

"Don't ever think of yourself as being less than someone else, my dear. You *are* who God created you to be. You can't let your family history control your destiny. He has a plan and a purpose for your life."

Ruth remembered hearing similar words from Mahlon back in Moab.

"All my fellow townsmen know that you are a woman of noble character," Boaz continued. "When you turned away from your false gods and confessed your allegiance to the God of Abraham, Isaac, and Jacob, God grafted you into His covenant people not in a physical sense but in a spiritual sense. That is what really matters for the here and now and for eternity."

Ruth wiped a tear. "Are you sure, my lord? I can't fathom such unconditional love."

Boaz said with emotion, "Neither can I, Ruth. I just accept it with gratitude. Believe me when I say, nothing would please me more than to redeem the land of Elimelech and Mahlon for you and Naomi. But I must inform you, there is a kinsman-redeemer who is closer kin than me. Although it would pain me greatly, it would only be right that he have the chance to redeem the land that Elimelech lost. If he is not willing, as surely as the Lord lives, I will do it. I would love to share with you what is in my heart, but I haven't the right to do that until this matter is resolved."

Ruth's heart soared when Boaz expressed his desire to marry her, but when she learned there was another kinsman-redeemer next in line, she was overcome by disappointment.

She let out a loud sigh, which ended in a quiet sob. She was tired and confused.

Boaz reached out his hand and gently wiped away her tears. His hand on her face felt like the touch of

God. She placed her hand over his and felt comforted. For now, that was enough.

With darkness surrounding him and Ruth, Boaz said, "Rest here until morning, my dear. Don't let it be known that you came to the threshing floor."

Feeling safe with Boaz, Ruth lay down and slept peacefully. Sometime before dawn, Boaz awakened her and said, "Bring me your shawl, and I will put barley in it. You must not go back to Naomi empty-handed."

In the early morning hour before sunrise, Ruth cautiously made her way back home. The fact that Boaz wanted to marry her made her heart sing, but knowing she might never know his love brought pain to her heart.

Love, real love, a godly love, is a beautiful thing, she remembered hearing Naomi say. *It can never be denied or forgotten.*

That's what she desired, a forever love, a godly love. However it turned out, she would accept God's plan and purpose for her life.

Walking up the path to the house, Ruth felt relief when she saw Naomi standing in the doorway.

"Mother, I'm home!"

Naomi hurried to her. "Tell me, Daughter, how did it go? I have been walking the floor, waiting for your return!"

"He didn't reject the idea of being our redeemer, Mother, but there is another kinsman next in line. Dare I hope the other man will not want to redeem us? I wonder how long I'll have to wait to find out if I can possibly have a future with Boaz. I won't be able to sleep until I know."

"You won't have to wait long, dear. I know Boaz. He's a man of his word. He will settle this matter today."

Ruth clutched her hands together. "Oh, Mother, I wish I knew the right words to pray."

"God hears our hearts, Ruth. Just talk to Him."

"You will find me in the garden, Mother. I'd like to be alone."

Chapter 15

A SANDAL AND A WEDDING

"So Boaz took Ruth and she became his wife" (Ruth 4:13).

Boaz was eager for sunrise. As soon as the sun came up and the village awoke, he made his way swiftly to the public square where the elders of the town gathered to take care of all legal transactions. He sat down and waited. When he saw the other kinsman walking by, he called to him.

"Darda! Shalom. Come over here, my friend, and sit down with me and the elders. I have something I want to discuss with you."

"Shalom, my friend. I'm listening."

They joined the ten elders on the bench. "I don't know if you have heard, but Naomi has returned from

Moab. The land that belonged to Elimelech is going to be sold," Boaz said.

"Yes, I know," Darda said with sarcasm in his voice. "I heard she had returned, bringing her Moabite daughter-in-law with her."

Boaz winced at his tone. *Oh, God, please intervene here.* Boaz could not bear the thought of this kinsman taking Ruth to be his wife.

Boaz continued, "As a close relative, you are first in line to buy the land. I thought I should bring the matter to your attention and suggest that you buy it in the presence of all seated here and in the presence of the elders of my people."

Darda stroked his beard, considering Boaz' words.

"If you wish to redeem the land, Darda, do so. But if you will not, tell me so I will know. No one has the right to it except you. Then I am next in line."

"I will redeem it," Darda said as he stood up and turned to the elders.

"It's your right. But there's one other thing," Boaz said. "Just so there is no misunderstanding about the transaction, on the day you redeem the land for Naomi and for Ruth the Moabitess, you acquire Mahlon's widow. In order to maintain the name of her dead husband with his property, if you have a son, he will bear the name of Mahlon."

"Now you just hold on," Darda said, shaking his head emphatically. "That sheds a different light on things! I can't buy it. It might endanger my own estate and my relationship with my own family. You buy it and take the Moabite widow with it! I don't wish to."

Boaz caught a quick breath and tried not to smile. "You know it is customary that in order to seal a legal transaction, you have to take off your sandal and give it to me. Are you willing to do that in the presence of these elders and other people?"

"Yes, I am." Darda reached down and removed his sandal and handed it to Boaz. "Here, take it!"

A crowd had gathered. In a loud voice, Boaz said: "All of you are witnesses today that I have bought from Naomi everything that belonged to Elimelech and Kilion and Mahlon, including responsibility for Ruth, the foreigner, the widow of Mahlon. It will be my honor to take her as my wife and keep the name of the deceased alive along with his inheritance. The memory and reputation of the deceased will not disappear out of his family or from his hometown. To all this, you are witnesses this very day."

The men around him said in unison, "Yes, we are witnesses!"

The presiding elder spoke in a very solemn voice. "May God make you famous in Bethlehem! May God make this woman who is coming into your household like Rachel and Leah, the two women who built the family of Israel. May your family be like the family of Perez, the son of Tamar."

It was done. Boaz left the public square, walking briskly. He was eager to see Ruth. He had longed for the day he could look into her beautiful eyes and express his love to her. But out of respect, he felt he should first go to Naomi with the good news.

With a bounce in his step, he hurried up to Naomi's house. He was glad to find her alone.

"Greetings, Naomi. I bring good news! It is settled. I will redeem the land belonging to Elimelech and your family and take Ruth as my wife . . . if you agree."

Naomi clapped her hands in delight. "If I agree? Boaz, you have made me a happy woman, but Ruth is the woman you need to be saying these things to. Go now; you will find her in the garden."

"First, Naomi, I want you to know how much I treasure her. She is everything I have longed for and waited for." His voice broke. "God has answered my prayer for a godly helpmate."

"God doesn't forget the dreams buried deep inside our hearts, Boaz. Go out to the garden and claim your future."

Boaz walked quickly to the garden area. He found Ruth pacing back and forth. He picked a blossom from a nearby Rose of Sharon and stood for a minute, taking in all her beauty.

"Shalom, Ruth."

She turned her head at the sound of Boaz's voice. "Shalom, Boaz."

"The other kinsman denied his right to redeem! God has answered our prayers, Ruth! My dearest, come here, and let me gaze into your eyes."

Ruth put her hand over her heart, looked up to heaven, and then let her joy carry her into the arms of Boaz.

He tucked the blossom behind her ear, took hold of her hand, and brought it to his lips. "Today, we will start making plans for a wedding feast," he said. "You *will* marry me, won't you? You haven't changed your mind, have you? I know you must have loved Mahlon, else you wouldn't have married him."

"You dear, sweet man. You have my heart . . . all of it," Ruth answered, blushing with excitement. "I will honor the memory of Mahlon forever, for he was my first love. But please understand that my love for you is different. It is a love ordained by God. There is no barrier between us. I shudder to think what I would have missed had it not been for Naomi's faithfulness to Jehovah God. I first heard of His sovereignty and covenant love from her."

"We have much for which to thank Naomi," Boaz said.

"I now have a question for you, my love. Why have you waited so long to marry? You could have had anyone you wanted."

"I haven't wanted anyone until I met you. God tells us to wait, and He will give us the desires of our hearts. It has been the desire of my heart to have a godly helpmate. I have waited for this day for such a long time. Let's start making plans for our wedding. Everyone in Bethlehem loves a reason to celebrate."

"I doubt that everyone will be celebrating, my lord," Ruth said with a laugh. "Some will be disappointed that you didn't choose them!"

"Ah, maybe so, but I have eyes only for you, my love." He reached up and caressed her beautiful face.

Tears of joy gathered in Ruth's eyes. "My darling Boaz, I'm so thankful you waited for God's timing. And I am so thankful that Jehovah God is a God of second chances."

"So am I." Boaz gently wiped away the tears that trickled down Ruth's face. "My beautiful bride to be, I love you with a *forever love*. Those whom God has joined together, we will let no one separate."

Their wedding took place a short time later. There was feasting and singing and dancing in the streets of Bethlehem for several days. Everyone celebrated with Boaz and Ruth: the rich and the poor, the young and the old.

People said it was a marriage made in heaven. Boaz took Ruth and Naomi to live with him. Of all the happy people, it was difficult to know who was the happiest—Boaz, Ruth, or Naomi.

Chapter 16

A BABY NAMED OBED

"Obed the father of Jesse, and Jesse the father of David"
(Ruth 4:22).

Months went by. Ruth and Naomi's days were filled with contentment. By God's gracious gift, Ruth conceived, and with the help of Liora, a son was born.

Liora turned to Naomi. "Praise be to the Lord, who this day has not left you without a kinsman-redeemer. May he become famous throughout Israel!"

Naomi's heart overflowed with a joy she had not known since her first child Mahlon was born.

Liora took the child from Ruth and handed him to Naomi. She counted every little finger and every little toe. She cooed and cuddled him against her breast.

There was no competition between Ruth and Naomi. There was enough love to go around.

Liora laid her hand on the newborn's forehead. "Naomi, this child will make you young again, my friend. He will renew your life and sustain you in your old age. I tell you, your precious daughter-in-law who loves you so much is worth more to you than seven sons."

"I couldn't agree more, Liora. I wouldn't trade her for the world," Naomi said through happy tears. "She gave up her homeland and her gods, came to a strange land, and God has rewarded her for her faithfulness to Him and to me."

When the seven days of seclusion required by Hebrew law were over, the house was filled with rejoicing. Everyone was eager to see this special child. Noise and laughter filled the house, the voices of many women talking and laughing.

Nava spoke up. "Ruth, we women have discussed it and have agreed that this little one should be named Obed. It means *servant*."

All the women in the room said with loud voices, "Amen and amen."

Ruth smiled.

Naomi's mind went back to the time when Liora had uttered what had become prophetic words: *Maybe God, in His time and in His providence, will bring something good from this sojourn in Moab.*

"This is indeed one of the most blessed days of my life," Naomi said.

Later that evening, as the door closed on the last guest, Ruth, Boaz, and Naomi sat together, enjoying the presence of little Obed.

Ruth looked to Naomi. "Mother," she said, "please bring me the small bag I brought from Moab."

With a puzzled look on his face, Boaz watched Naomi leave the room and return with a small bag. Ruth opened it and brought out a cup the size a child would drink from.

"So this was the bulge in the bottom of your bag!" Naomi said.

"Yes, Grandmother. Mahlon made it. It was to be used by the son he would have someday. It is yours. Take it and treasure it." She handed Naomi the cup. "Boaz, come here, my love. By Hebrew law, Obed is Mahlon's heir and will bear Mahlon's name, but he is your son, born of our 'forever love.' "

With great tenderness, Ruth placed little Obed in the arms of Boaz.

As he cradled Obed in his arms, he looked heavenward and said with emotion in his voice, "This precious little boy is a fulfillment of a generational blessing that God has bestowed upon all of us."

Tears filled his eyes and trickled down his cheeks as he remembered Elimelech's last words to him: *I hope my sons grow up to be the man you are.*

He then lifted Obed close to his heart and prayed aloud. "Oh, Lord, most high and holy—please help me to walk in a manner worthy of this cherished child. When he looks at me, may he see a reflection of Your love for him."

Naomi could not contain her joy. "Ruth! Boaz! Wouldn't it be wonderful if someday it were to be recorded that our little Obed was in the generational line from which the Promised One came?"

Boaz squeezed the hand of Ruth and smiled. "Naomi, we will leave *that* in the hands of Almighty God and His plan and purpose for Obed's life."

"And we know that in all things God works for the good of those who love him, who have been called according to his purpose"

(Romans 8:28).

EPILOGUE

God had a plan for Naomi's life, and He watched over her during the lonely years she spent in Moab. And God had a plan for Ruth, the beautiful girl from Moab who chose to follow Naomi's God. And God certainly had a plan for the little baby Obed, born to Ruth and Boaz.

Hundreds of years later, the writer of sacred history would include in the genealogy of Jesus Christ: "*Salmon the father of Boaz, whose mother was Rahab, Boaz the father of Obed, whose mother was Ruth, Obed the father of Jesse, and Jesse the father of King David*" (Matthew 1:5-6).

And God has a plan for your life. Even if you have failed in the past and your life has been broken, God is the God of second chances. He specializes in mending broken vessels.

"Jesus answered, "I am the way and the truth and the life. No one comes to the Father except through me"

(John 14:6).

A FINAL WORD

When we trust Jesus Christ as our Savior and commit our lives to follow Him, we receive forgiveness of our sins and eternal life. His Spirit comes to live within us to help us. The Word of God says, *"In the same way, the Spirit helps us in our weakness"* (Romans 8:26).

God wants us to grow as believers in Christ and become stronger in our faith. We grow as believers by reading the Word of God and by praying each day. We should praise Him for His goodness and kindness and thank Him for His blessings to us.

It is not always easy to follow Jesus. We should not be surprised when others give us a hard time because we are believers in Christ. Jesus said, *"If they persecuted me, they will persecute you also. . . . They will treat you this way because of my name, for they do not know the One who sent me"* (John 15:20-21).

Love and forgiveness should characterize our lives as believers even in the face of persecution. Jesus said, *"But I tell you: Love your enemies and pray for those who persecute you"* (Matthew 5:44).

When Jesus was dying on the cross, He prayed for those who were putting Him to death. He prayed, *"Father, forgive them, for they do not know what they are doing"* (Luke 23:34).

We do not face persecution alone. God knows about every trial we face, and He is with us. God has said, *"Never will I leave you; never will I forsake you"* (Hebrews 13:5).

May you bask in God's "Forever Love."

"Have I not commanded you? Be strong and courageous. Do not be terrified; do not be discouraged, for the Lord your God will be with you wherever you go"

(Joshua 1:9).

GROUP DISCUSSION QUESTIONS

1. There was a famine in the land of Judah. What did Boaz mean when he indicated there was also a famine of the soul? Have you ever experienced this?

....

2. Can you sympathize with Elimelech for the predicament he faced during the famine? Were his choices understandable?

....

3. Have you ever faced a situation that required you to choose between God's directions and your own desire? What was the outcome?

....

4. How important is it to keep good company? How do you feel about the story of the frog in the pot? Have you been there?

....

5. Why did God discourage the Israelites from associating with the Moabites?

    ....

6. Do you pray for guidance before making plans, or do you pray for God to bless the plans you have already made?

    ....

7. The friendship between Liora and Naomi was a special kind of relationship. How important do you think it is to have a trusted friend to talk to?

    ....

8. Elimelech and Naomi experienced culture shock upon seeing all the idols in Moab. Do you have any idols? If so, what are they? What are our country's idols?

    ....

9. What do you think about Elimelech's deathbed cry: "May God forgive me"? Do you believe God forgave him?

    ....

10. Have you ever had a loved one taken who left you without a song to sing? Did you blame God, others, or yourself? What enabled you to let go and move on?

    ....

11. What lesson did you learn from the relationship between Naomi and her daughters-in-law?

....

12. Ruth saw something different in Naomi that made her want what she had. Are you a difference maker?

....

13. Did you see God's sovereignty at work in Ruth's life? What about Orpah's life?

....

14. What was the deciding factor in Ruth's decision to go with Naomi?

....

15. What is it like to hold on to a dream? Do you see the importance of waiting for God's timing?

....

16. Have you ever felt less than someone? What helped you to overcome this feeling?

....

17. What traits of character do you most admire in Ruth? In Boaz? In Naomi?

....

18. Are you still looking for your Ruth . . . your Boaz?

....

19. Can you recall a time when you felt God calling you to make a significant change? How did you respond? Do you now see the upheaval as being used by God?

....

20. Because of his mother, Rahab, Boaz understood that God's grace is greater than all our sins. Have you experienced the joy of a second chance?

....

21. Obed was David's grandfather. Jesus was from the line of David. What message do you get from that? God's faithfulness? God's providence? God's sovereignty? All three?

....

22. Looking back . . . are you able to trace God's plan and purpose in your life?

....

23. Can you see yourself in the story of Ruth . . . broken and in need of a kinsman-redeemer?

....

*"Trust in the Lord with all
your heart
and lean not on your own
understanding;
in all your ways acknowledge
him,
and he will make your
paths straight"*
(Proverbs 3:5-6).

"But those who hope in the
Lord
will renew their strength.
They will soar on wings like
eagles;
they will run and not grow
weary,
they will walk and not be
faint"
(Isaiah 40:31).

ACKNOWLEDGEMENTS

This book would not have been possible without the help and encouragement of those whom God has placed on my path as I have followed my dream to publication.

....

My unending gratitude to Ruth Bochte . . . I've watched her grow from a young teenager to a godly wife and mother. Isn't it just like God to provide a modern day "Ruth" who has chosen to use her God-inspired illustrations to help bring this story to life?

....

To my nephew and fellow writer Dr. Jeff Sibley, who encouraged me to follow my dream: You believed I could publish before I believed it myself.

....

To Debbie Carter, my Sunday school teacher, and her husband, Neal, the director of missions at my church: Thank you for your prayers, encouragement, and helpful suggestions. To me, you two are a present-day Ruth and Boaz.

To Larry Alston, President of Christ to the World Ministries: You opened a door that allowed me to write Bible studies and Bible dramas that are spreading God's Word into many countries via radio and other means. Your vision for reaching the world for Christ became my vision also.

I would be remiss if I did not mention my granddaughter Cortney, who years ago first introduced me to a computer. She ran down the hill from her house to mine many times to help me with problems (and there were many) that challenged me.

To Sonia Burden: I thank you for answering numerous technical questions with patience and expertise.

To Jennifer Hallmark: I thank you for sharing your knowledge and helpful ideas on fiction writing.

....

Thanks to all who read my book and graciously wrote reviews. I appreciate you.

....

I welcome this space to honor the memory of my dear friend Janice Wynn, who invited me to my first Southern Christian Writers Conference at Samford University in Birmingham, Alabama, many years ago. God used her to open up a whole new world for me.

....

To my siblings and their families: You have given me much to write about during my lifetime. Relax . . . I wouldn't dare tell it all.

....